The Down and Outs

The Down and Outs

A Journey through a Female Attack Victim's Eyes during the Aftermath of Her Ordeal

Karen Clark

authorHOUSE®

AuthorHouse™ UK Ltd.
1663 Liberty Drive
Bloomington, IN 47403 USA
www.authorhouse.co.uk
Phone: 0800.197.4150

This is a work of fiction. All of the characters, names, incidents, organizations, and dialogue in this novel are either the products of the author's imagination or are used fictitiously.

Published by AuthorHouse   05/15/2013

ISBN: 978-1-4817-9463-3 (sc)
ISBN: 978-1-4817-9464-0 (hc)
ISBN: 978-1-4817-9465-7 (e)

Any people depicted in stock imagery provided by Thinkstock are models, and such images are being used for illustrative purposes only.
Certain stock imagery © Thinkstock.

This book is printed on acid-free paper.

Chapter One

Above the earth's narrow horizon rose the sun to shine upon a restructured, 'sedated' society. Somewhere on the busy globe existed England which, like everywhere else, had been neatly divided into five separate sections. Four Hemispheres covered most of the country; the remainder being the 'Non-Hemisphere'—a drab, unprosperous quarter where the 'Down and Outs' lived.

In the great 'cleansing' which had followed the riots, the Down and Outs were placed at the bottom of the heap; they were the outcasts, rejected by society. A great number of them were semi-educated, while many more could neither read nor write.

The Non-Hemisphere was made up of a number of lanes bordered by shacks in clusters that resembled villages; anachronisms choosing to be left behind in their ways. At either end of the Non-Hemisphere was a labyrinth leading obscurely into the Hemispheres. Separated from the Non-Hemisphere by one of these labyrinths was Terminal Lane; a horse-shoe cul-de-sac from which a crooked pathway descended steeply to the sea. Sometimes, at dusk, a cluster of Non-Hemisphere Down and Outs could be seen sitting listlessly on the beach there, watching the waves rising in splendour, only to collapse shattered on the shore, like emblems of their own misfortune. Into the crash of foam and crossing water some broken-hearted clown would wade and let the strong tide bowl him over and over.

In their homes, the fires of the Down and Outs did not warm them; their curtains concealed secrets not worth hiding; on their dull walls hung no medallions or certificates of fame. The inns of this quarter were chapels in disguise. There the Non-Hemisphere inhabitants went to pour out their hearts, not in prayer but in jealous gossip of the privileged denizens of the Hemispheres to which they aspired in vain. Hardened, proud spinsters who had, at one time, worked for their living, and who claimed to be feminists, boasted about their diligence and independence; under their confident existence lurked the wounds that would not heal. Each had a story to tell of how she had been snubbed and scorned by the ruthless businessmen of the Northern Hemisphere where, for a few months, she had taken herself to work. Those who had striven to better themselves in this way had all suffered the same fate of ultimate scorn and dismissal. Their humbler sisters who stayed at home, degenerated into slovens by the more direct route.

Along the amber shore aimlessly glided one who, at first glance, seemed to have everything going for her. She was a young woman, pure of face and slender; her long black hair glowed reddish in this light. She walked composedly, wrapping her shawl around her against the cold; but for all her apparent gentleness, she too harboured an injured spirit; she too was an outcast.

She made her way back to the cottage which she called home, where she found her aunt standing by the decrepit gas stove in the kitchen, making soup.

"You've been a long time," remarked the old body, stirring busily.

"I wanted to get some fresh air," the younger woman replied. "It makes me feel more relaxed."

The aunt instantly let go of the ladle and turned to face her niece. "You've plenty of time to feel relaxed now you're out of that job in the Northern Hemisphere, Kate."

The young woman ignored the sting of criticism and replied bitterly: "Why didn't you warn me about what would happen, Aunt Nancy? You could see what was coming; you should have told me. I am your niece, after all."

Aunt Nancy's brows drew down into a tighter frown; it was her only sign of emotion. "One 'as to find out about life oneself, doesn't one?" she said. "No one never told me before *I* went to work there."

"No," retorted Kate, "and the experience doesn't seem to have affected you much. But it's done long-term damage to me, and I think you know that."

"So, these things happen." Her aunt shrugged nonchalantly. "We're Non-Hemisphere; what can we expect? It's the system, girl; it's what we're brought up to."

Kate took off her shawl and flung it over the back of the nearest chair. "Yes, Aunt Nancy," she retorted peevishly, "but I wasn't brought up to it, don't forget; I can't take these things lying down."

"You was unlucky, girl," said her aunt, setting a battered soup bowl before her on the table. "But remember this: if it 'adn't been for me, you wouldn't 'ave a roof over your 'ead."

Kate sat down resignedly to face her breakfast. She had long since learnt how useless it was to accuse her aunt of not caring about her; given the least chance, she would trot out the same old argument as before.

She thought of the Eastern Hemisphere, the quarter in which she had been born and where she had lived up until the age of sixteen. It was a magnificent quarter; a land of forts and watchtowers; of white marble villages and mosaic-encrusted temples; of neat towns encompassed by strong stone walls. Writers and artists, musicians and scholars, teachers and sportsmen lived there; the Eastern Hemisphere colour was gold, symbolic of wealth and triumph. Beyond the walls of some of its larger towns stood great amphitheatres to which the populace would flock to cheer on their favourite runners and vaulters as they toiled in the race. Every spring without fail, the teams from the Eastern Hemisphere would return home victorious from the International Olympic Games held at a stadium in the middle of the Four Hemispheres. Their uniform was golden, and golden were the medals which hung around their necks.

And here, in the late twenty-first century, in the poverty and squalor of the Non-Hemisphere sat Kate Brannigan, banished from all that glory. Six years ago, after training for a career, she had found herself a post as a Shorthand / Typist in the Northern Hemisphere; and six months after that her dream of redemption was brutally shattered.

The Northern Hemisphere was represented by the colour red. It was the home of businessmen, politicians and white-collar workers; a cut-throat world whose inhabitants specialised in carving one another up. Ruthless and sophisticated, their minds were razor-sharp, and Kate could still feel the throb of scars they had inflicted on her when she attempted to work amongst them.

Kate had not been alone in her endeavour to break out from the unemployed masses of the Non-Hemisphere; in her day, many other teenage girls had gone to train for office posts in the prosperous Northern Hemisphere. Barely a kilometre away from Terminal Lane, the Northern Hemisphere was seen as endlessly attractive to their kind; they were prepared to tolerate the inevitable insults in the hope of self-advancement.

Kate sighed as she remembered the two-faced businessmen she had once worked for. They were life assurance representatives, armed invisibly with sharp knives, and with substantial briefcases. The entire office atmosphere reeked of hierarchy and sophistication.

Everyone appeared to be friendly, cracking the occasional joke. The girls gave the impression that they enjoyed typing letters in which the same sentence constantly recurred, and dealing with recalcitrant customers on the telephone. But if they managed to keep the tedium which they felt out of their faces, there was no room for spontaneous enjoyment, for their clothes and wages were of fairly modest quality. But boredom will out in spite of all disguises; in their case, it emerged in the vapid set phrases which they used—a kind of staccato language without depth or feeling, like something pouring endlessly off a production line.

The representatives, on the other hand, were quick-tempered and aggressive; they wore their arrogance as naturally as their suits. Often they would enter the office after having been snubbed by a client; and attempt to provoke an argument with the first office worker in sight. If the worker complained to someone higher up, he or she would simply be told that the representatives were under enormous pressure, and that it was a natural reaction on their parts to become short-tempered and irritable. It was noticeable, however, how these same men contrived not to be offensive to their own superiors; with them they would strive to be as charming as possible, in order to convey the impression that they were very much in control.

The office workers, particularly the women, were not supposed to express their opinions. The male office workers were sometimes allowed to joke and make personal remarks to the representatives; but if their female colleagues attempted the same familiarity, they risked being ignored or being told politely to mind their manners. Such was the code in the Northern Hemisphere working environment. It made Kate squirm even to think about it.

She shuddered too, as she remembered how differently the representatives treated their wives. It was almost as if each one were in the grip of a kind of schizophrenia, making them tyrants in the office and gentle giants at home. Her mind went back to an incident involving one particular representative, Mr Richards, whom she remembered as having snapped at everyone except the manager and his dear, helpless wife.

It was only her second month in employment as a Shorthand / Typist to twenty life assurance representatives in the Northern Hemisphere, but she was already beginning to regret ever having accepted the post. At eleven thirty one morning, Kate could remember timidly rising from her desk to answer an incoming call from the switchboard, whose constant buzzing reverberated in your ears from the moment you set foot in the office to the moment you left it. The caller, as she quickly realised from his grating voice, was none other than Mr Richards himself. She would have preferred it to have been a client, as all her previous dealings with Mr Richards had been marked by acerbity and unpleasant behaviour on his part. Now again, he dealt out more of the same.

"I came into the office earlier on," he told her brusquely, "but I had to rush home because the telephone man has to fix the wire and I have to hold it while he fixes it into the socket."

In the background Kate could hear his silly wife bleating about something. It amazed her that a man like Mr Richards could be so sharp with herself, and yet so comparatively mild and forgiving with that absurd creature. But she restrained herself and answered sweetly:

"And you would like me to let the manager know that you'll be in later?"

"Of course I would," snapped an irate Mr Richards. "You don't think I'm phoning you for fun, do you? If I'm forced to rush home and interrupt my work, I have to inform the manager. It figures, doesn't it?"

Kate felt the looming presence of her supervisor at her shoulder, and knew that she was waiting to pounce. Nevertheless, she was a girl of spirit and had to speak her mind.

"Quite frankly, no, it doesn't," she said, sighing with disgust.

"What's that comment supposed to mean?" hissed the angry voice at the other end of the line.

"Oh, I'd have thought it would have been quite obvious," replied Kate, keeping her back to the supervisor. "Your wife's at home, isn't she? Why on earth can't she hold the telephone wire herself? I just can't understand why you travel twenty miles from the office, when she's sitting around doing nothing."

"For Heaven's sake, Kate!" barked the impatient representative. "I'm anxious that the manager knows why I'll be slightly delayed today. Now, are you going to pass on the message or not?"

Kate felt the predatory footsteps of her supervisor creeping closer. "Perhaps you could have held the wire while your wife passed the message on," she retorted, with a trace of sarcasm in her voice.

But she knew at once that she had gone too far. Even before Mr Richards had a chance to reply, the supervisor stepped in, curt and dismissive.

"All right, Kate," she said, taking the receiver. "I'll handle the call."

Obviously there had been a secret meeting and a quiet complaint, for after that, she was never in demand to take any of the representatives' calls. It was then that she realised that her days at the 'Diamond Life Assurance' company were numbered.

Another instance had more directly concerned a representative's wife; in this case Mrs Sarah White. Mr White was a huge, hard-faced man in his mid-thirties, whose voice resembled the barking of a bloodhound; whereas his wife was of medium height, slim and attractive. It was her common practice, like many of these ladies, to waltz into the office luxuriously adorned in a fur coat, her small, simian face smeared with make-up. She put on lofty airs, but underneath it all she seemed pleasant and rather timid.

Kate, however, could perceive that this woman was not made of butter. Her husband's character was written on his face; he could have been bred especially for his cut-throat profession. He reeked of superciliousness, and sneered at everyone, including even the manager who, however, did not rebuke him for it. Perhaps he mistook his rudeness for strength of character.

Sarah was often at the office or would telephone from home whenever she required her husband's assistance. Even when Mr White was busy, his wife's pretty pleadings seemed to win him over. After the hubbub of shouting scenes in the office, Kate used to be infuriated by the meek complaisant tone he would put on for his wife's benefit. He was always telling her to 'take care'; but what care did he take when his hopeful employees were put out of a job after a few months?

As she ate, Kate scanned the tiny kitchen where she sat. All around her there was nothing but creviced walls, chipped paint, shabby neglected furniture, and the general atmosphere of poverty so typical of the Non-Hemisphere. She reflected how her aunt tolerated and indeed hardly seemed to notice such things. She had been brought up in this quarter and knew it like the back of her wrinkled hand; she breathed its air and shared its inhabitants' rough speech and peasant ways. And now Kate, though she hated herself for it, found she was lapsing into the same faults. It was shameful, but what could she do? She was a prisoner without any prospect of release. She had been forced to herd with these debased people whose colour green aptly conveyed the envy which flowed through their veins.

Chapter Two

"You must come with me on my next visit to the gymnasium," Kate's father said jovially, as they sat on the long veranda facing the garden of their Eastern Hemisphere villa. "I can teach you how to defend yourself."

"What me?" laughed Kate. "You can try, Father, but I doubt if I'd even be able to fend a midget off."

Kate's father searched her face anxiously. "Oh, you'd be surprised, Kate. Women are stronger than they know. All you need is to actually believe that you're capable of it. Come on, give it a try—for my sake, eh? It may prove useful one day."

The veranda overlooked the courtyard which was adorned with multi-coloured gladioli and tranquil fountains. In the light of the setting sun, the cascading pulses of water turned a radiant, Eastern Hemisphere gold.

"But martial arts don't interest me, Father," said the girl. "Mother never bothered to learn, and she does all right."

But at the mention of her mother, Kate noticed with pain her father's wistful golden eyes turned from her to gaze along the sun-drenched patio. The sun sank lower; all of a sudden, the fountains pumped danger, their columns of water spurting like blood from a severed artery. She had never known him to react so anxiously to her opinions before, and for the first time in her life she fearfully sensed that he had lost control in some way.

"Father," she stammered, placing an earnest hand upon his arm, "something's wrong, isn't it?" It concerns Mother, doesn't it?" she persisted when he did not reply. "I've noticed the way she's been acting lately. She's become strange, cold and distant. Oh, Father, I'm scared! Please don't shut me out! Tell me what it is."

He brought his hand round to grip hers tightly, and drew her head down to his chest. "Oh, Kate! Kate!" he said softly. "I've been trying to keep this from you for so long, but I might have known I couldn't do so forever. You're a child still, but you're growing up so quickly and you're bound to notice certain things. It's true. There's been a rift between your mother and myself for some time, and now I'm afraid she's decided that things can't go on. I love you both dearly, but I cannot continue to live in this household for much longer."

Kate sat up, staring at him, troubled and not understanding. "But why, Father?" she pleaded. "Why can't you stay? I love you."

"It's not as simple as that, Kate", he replied sadly. "Your mother and I are now barely on speaking terms. It would not be fair to you, to any of us, to carry on as we are. I've thought about it hard and long, and this way seems to me the only right one."

"But, Father," cried Kate, feeling her happy and safe world breaking up around her, "where will you go?"

"There's a villa to the south of the Eastern Hemisphere," he said unsteadily. "It stands near the forum, close by a temple. I've been to look at it a few times, and I've decided to make it my future home. You shall come to visit me once I have settled in." The sun had now sunk completely. The chilly fingers of the night were stealing up; still they sat on. "But it will not be a permanent home, like this one is," his voice continued bleakly. "I have signed up as a legionary."

Kate was appalled. "A foot-soldier?" she murmered. "Father—your life will be constantly in danger!"

There was a silence between them. Perhaps he had not heard her, for when he resumed it was not in response to her frightened cry. "As you know, I have friends who are soldiers. There's Julius, a splendid fellow, and Honorius also. When we're not campaigning, I can live among them in the fort. It'll not be like going into the outer darkness. The fort has shops and temples. There will be plenty to keep me occupied until I return to my villa. Things will take their course, Kate," he said soothingly, though she did not believe his calm. "Life will soon pick up again after I'm gone. And they won't be so bad for me, either. You'll see."

She remembered how she had not slept that night, but had lain staring up at the patterned ceiling of her bedroom, her father's sad words resounding in her head. Suddenly it seemed to her that her childhood was ending.

The atmosphere in the household did not improve in the fortnight that followed. Kate's mother remained distant and inscrutable, repelling all attempts at intimacy. Kate herself felt constrained and awkward, like one bearing a heavy load which weighed down her every step.

Then had come that dismal autumn morning when, stealing into the lounge, she had found her father bundling some of his belongings into a suitcase. At first, she had stood back concealing herself, while those precious, elusive articles burned into her brain. There was his white linen toga, its hem woven in dazzling, Eastern Hemisphere gold, which he would sometimes wear to work; and that familiar, black tunica for less formal occasions; plus the various other garments he possessed. A hot tear trickled slowly down her cheek, as she watched him lift a little wooden bowl to his lips and kiss it tenderly before wrapping it in tissue paper to keep it safe on his journey. She recognised the bowl; it was an ornament she had given him for his birthday when she was still at infant school. He tucked it between the clothes in his suitcase, with a few photographs of herself and her mother.

Then he turned and saw her; their eyes met and Kate came forward. She saw, not for the first time how like his eyes were to her own, though of a lighter shade. That was inevitable, because she was a part of himself; an extension of his very existence.

"When do you leave, Father?" she asked softly.

"This evening," he said. "The warship sails at eight o'clock. I'll be going straight into battle."

"So soon?" she gasped. "I didn't think you'd be going to war just yet. I thought you'd need some time to . . ." She swallowed hard, but the lump in her throat would not go. ". . . to get over all this."

He shook his head. "No, Kate. It will help take my mind off things. Besides," he added, with a touch of bitterness, "it makes no difference anymore."

Kate had to breathe deeply to stop herself from bursting into tears. It was the last thing she wanted; she desired above all not to embarrass her father or make things any more difficult for him than they already were. A vision of the little wooden bowl kept flashing before her eyes. It swelled in her mind until it took over the shape of the entire lounge. Then it vanished as, with a click, he shut the lid of the suitcase. Her mother, like an automaton, came into the room.

"Breakfast will be served in ten minutes," she said.

Kate ran out into the courtyard and threw up.

That evening, the golden shore, greying as night came on, felt unsteady beneath Kate's feet. Her mother stood silently beside her, seemingly unmoved. Kate's eyes were pinned on her father. He was speaking to Julius while he carried his luggage on board the 'Titan'. She remembered wondering what they were talking about—strategic affairs, perhaps. For Julius's position was an important one. As standard-bearer, he was responsible for leading his soldiers into battle; he was a step up from her father in rank. Presumably they were discussing the latter's battle duties in advance; but there was no way of being certain.

Kate glanced gloomily at her watch. It was a few minutes before eight o'clock. She saw Julius turn his brave, regal head in her direction, adorned in the leopard skin headdress of the standard-bearer. Her father came back on shore with another legionary (whom she later learned to be Honorius) to bid herself and her mother farewell. Though the darkness was encroaching with giant strides, his breastplate and helmet flashed bright bronze in her eyes. It was an image to store away in the depths of her brain, like that of the little wooden bowl; they were keepsakes celebrating the invisible bond between father and daughter.

The two soldiers drew nearer, their polished leather tunics flapping in the autumn breeze. Honorius halted tactfully at a distance, while Kate's father marched bravely on. He approached his wife first.

"Goodbye, Miriam," he said, firmly but sincerely. It was noticeable that there was no physical contact. She looked for a trace of sadness on her mother's face; there was none that she could see.

"Goodbye, Andronicus."

Kate felt herself trembling. She looked down at her feet; the shadow of her father's shield, and the tip of his spear merged with that of her shocked and aching body. "I'll teach you how to defend yourself," he had said just before this upheaval. But now the silver moon mocked her with its light. "Too late! Too late!" She fought back the tears as her father drew near, taking her hand in his.

"Don't forget," he told her. "My new village in Colchester. You must come and stay there for a few weeks on my return." He stroked her hair gently. "Look after your mother for me. God bless, Kate." He kissed her on one cheek. "God bless," he repeated; his voice echoed across the cool, shadowed shore.

He never did return. The following spring, when the legionaries marched back, dishevelled, just out of battle, Andronicus was not among them. Julius came to the villa to break the news to Kate and her mother. He had been killed on the third day of fighting. Honorius had been wounded, but it was said that he would recover. Kate's mother cried a little, but composed herself shortly afterwards, offering Julius a seat and a goblet of wine. He, who had once been close, now sounded distant and cold.

"I am not here to celebrate, Miriam." There was a trace of hostility in his narrow, grey eyes. "However, I thank you for your hospitality." He turned to leave; then, hesitating, he faced round again. He was holding a long wooden spear, tipped with iron, which Kate remembered her father referring to as a 'pilum', a legionary's basic weapon.

"I almost forgot," and he held the pilum out to Kate. "Careful, it's very sharp. This was your father's weapon, Kate. He requested that you keep it just before he died."

Kate's mother looked baffled, and uncomfortable; Julius was excluding her deliberately, as they both knew. She fiddled with the fringes of her stola.

"I have some urgent matters to attend to," he went on brusquely. "I bid you good day." Then he marched out through the front door and out of their lives. He never came to the villa again.

Kate remembered sitting that night on the veranda, clutching her father's pilum to her stola. She sensed that he had given it to her for a purpose, and she connected it in her mind with his having wanted her to learn to defend herself. She held out the spear horizontally in both hands. It was not unlike the arrows that she and her father had used when they practised archery together, although without the flights obviously.

Turning from the railings of the veranda, as if to retire to her room, she suddenly felt the tears which she had held back for so long pricking her eyes. She thought of the evening of her father's departure, and looked up at the harsh, gibbous moon. Smugly, it seemed to convey to her that she was crying alone. She lashed out at it in frustration, and went to her bedroom. For days afterwards she was plunged in floods of tears.

Chapter Three

But there were, too, memories of a different kind. One glorious Saturday in July, three months after she had lost her father, would never fade from her thoughts.

She had asked her mother if she would join her at archery practice in the courtyard. But her mother, it appeared, had already planned to spend the weekend at a friend's villa in Chester. Rebecca, a friend from school, happened to be on holiday in Cyprus that particular week. Pity; her presence might have saved her from unsuspected dangers.

Without companion or competitor, the growing Kate gave way to other impulses. Her body was filling out; she had a woman's curves, though her mind was still childlike. Viewing herself in the mirror gave her pleasant thoughts. On this day, she found herself in her room, slipping into her best stola and adorning her young face with cosmetics which, until now, had lain intact amidst the contents of her dressing table drawer.

Her father had promised to take her to the Southern Hemisphere the summer before he died. Kate had never visited this quarter, but from reports it sounded to be a vast and mysterious land. Farmers, clergymen and doctors were its inhabitants; its colour was soft, a subtle mauve. White churches stood amongst its golden fields; there were plush hotels, too, and nightclubs, for it attracted tourists even from the affluent East. For Kate, the very world 'nightclub' had the allure of forbidden fruit.

Two approaches to the quarter were possible: on foot via the labyrinth, or by the Electro-Train, for which a ticket had to be bought. This flew attached to an electric cable, high above the towns, and went so swiftly that the journey would not exceed three quarters of an hour. It was Kate's choice.

She slipped her gold-threaded palla over her head and shoulders, securing it with a bronze oval brooch which reflected the sun. Gazing at her reflection in the dressing table mirror, she thought that she might pass for sixteen, which was the minimum age for entering most nightclubs. In fact, she would be sixteen in December, a matter of a mere five months away. She did not consult her mother; she was not in the mood to welcome moral advice, perhaps least of all from that source. Indeed, over only one item did she hesitate, and that was her 'disguisive' mac of shiny crimson plastic, which hung on a hook on her bedroom door. Everybody—Hemisphere and Non-Hemisphere inhabitants alike—had one of these, its purpose being as an all-enveloping garment to conceal one's origin and lessen friction whenever one travelled out of one's hemisphere. But to Kate, at this moment, it seemed like one more clog of parental restriction, and deliberately, she left it behind.

She decided to make her way to the Electro-Terminus by way of the forum. Evening was already coming on, and its soft yellow glow was like the relaxing focus of a sleepy eye. The crowds in the great market-place were dispersing; the traders were already packing away.

As she reached the forum exit, she halted and turned back, her attention caught by an object on one of the few remaining stalls. It was a ring made of zinc; but that was not the fascination. It was serpentine in shape, with a knot at the end of its tail; its deep, hypnoptic eyes staring back at Kate were of unfathomable onyx. It was a little overpriced, but it fitted her finger perfectly; so she happily forked out the money and hurried on. She reached the Electro-Station ticket office a few minutes later.

"Could I have a return ticket to the Southern Hemisphere, please?" she said eagerly to the man behind the counter—a large, burly black with a pipe stuck in his mouth.

"Er—which section were yer wanting, Miss?" he asked, through swirls of tobacco smoke. She guessed he must be from the Western Hemisphere, where the blue-collar and transport workers lived.

"I'm not sure," she replied hesitantly. "I was hoping to go to one of the Southern Hemisphere nightclubs."

"Was yer now?" said the ticket man, removing the pipe from his lips and staring at her intently. "Going alone?"

"Yes." Kate was uncertain as to whether she should be offended by his curiosity.

He dropped his gaze to the ticket machine before him. "You'll be out in the sticks," he commented. "Right the way out to the Farmlands section. Them nightclubs are scattered about there."

"Is it *that* far from here?" she enquired, rather concerned.

"Farther than from its two neighbouring sections," replied the ticket man, still not activating the machine.

"How much, please?"

"Oh, it ain't the expense of it, Miss," he said. "It's just that them kind of nightclubs ain't no places for young ladies of your sort." His tone was admonitory; indeed, too painfully reminiscent of her mother. She overrode his objections, bought the ticket and stepped into the communal lift which carried her, with many others, to the platforms of the Electro-Terminus. She followed the signs which lead her on to Platform 7 (C), guided by notices in large, mauve letters which read: "THE SOUTHERN HEMISPHERE LINE: THE MEDICO: THE SYNOD AND THE FARMLANDS—STRAIGHT

AHEAD". Then she sat down on one of the plastic seats to wait, her eyes drifting to the faded metropolis below. She could barely spot her villa; it looked tiny beside the great bulk of the Basilica. She played with her ring and the snake emblem stared back at her.

Nearby were a few Western Hemisphere people wearing the red mac over the traditional blue overalls of their quarter. Three in particular came to sit on the same seat with her. She did not pay them much more attention, until one of them, a skinny, downtrodden looking man, apparently of Asian extract began to speak:

"All set for the 'Rhythm & Blues' then, Fritz? He grinned sheepishly towards one of his companions, a black who was carrying a suitcase and a toolbox.

"You bet, man," replied the man so addressed. "I's had 'nough of hammering them blasted nails into them walls that is falling to bits. Give me the Farmlands every day o' the year; then I's be happy."

"There's not all the much difference between the Farmlands and our Western Hemisphere, though, Fitzroy," struck in the third man. "Except that the Farmlands look more posh, and has all those open fields."

"Ah, but them nightclubs, Jim," Fitzroy persisted, leaning back and closing his eyes meditatively. "There ain't no place like them. Mauve liquor; rhythm and blues; all them chicks waitin' to be picked up . . . Man, that's the life."

Kate felt a faint twinge of unease; but she continued to listen to the three labourers' conversation.

"It's the Medico for me for next year's holiday," said Jim. "There's a few nightclubs around there, too, I believe. They may be well worth visiting."

"Getting ideas above our station, are we, Jim?" asked the Asian truculently. "The Farmlands not good enough for you, or somethin'?"

"Oh, they're all right, I guess," replied Jim. "I just don't see any harm in a change now and then, that's all."

"You wait till you get there, boy, and you'll soon see the harm," the Indian came back strongly. "The Medico? You may be better speaking than what we are, but as soon as they find out you're from the Western Hemisphere, they'll tell you their 'otels are fully booked. I know, boy. Me and me mate fell right into that trap a couple of years ago."

"Same here, Gerry," struck in Fitzroy.

"The Medico may not refuse to treat us when we go there for illnesses," continued the Asian, "but whenever it comes to us livin' amongst them, we're rubbish—they don't want to know. Stick to your own kind, Jim. People from the Synod and the Medico are nothin' but a load of insular snobs."

The loudspeakers sprang into life at this moment, announcing the approach of the electro-train, and their conversation was interrupted. Soon enough, the train itself came gliding into the sleepy station, illuminating it with its dazzling neon lights. The three blue-collar workers rose briskly and so did Kate.

"Here it is, folks!" proclaimed Fitzroy cheerfully, "All aboard!" They clambered into one of the cylindrical, streamlined carriages and Kate entered the one behind.

Half an hour later the Electro-Train reached the Medico section of the Southern Hemisphere quarter. By now the sun had lost its potency and was withdrawing from the sky. It was eight o'clock. A few passengers got off here, but no one entered Kate's carriage, she noticed. As they drew rapidly out of the station, the surrounding scenery of hospitals and semi-detached dwellings gradually gave way to a mass of spired churches, white in colour, but already beginning to be veiled in darkness. This religious concentration continued until they pulled into THE SYNOD station, which was decorated with neon, multi-coloured crucifixes.

It was half past eight by the illuminated clock on the platform wall. Kate looked about her, as the aluminium doors zoomed shut. In spite of being alone in the carriage, she felt the adrenalin pumping through her body as the Electro-Train glided forward, ready to transport her into the land of the unknown. She leant against the window with excited, eager eyes, watching the spires thin out until no more were to be seen. For a few minutes an emptiness succeeded, which began to be punctuated with scattered thatched houses along rural lanes; apart from the odd shabby farmhouse, the landscape became one of large open fields. Still Kate sat patiently, waiting for the vibrant metropolis of her dreams to begin. However, as the Electro-Train sped on its way, her happy smile began to wear thin.

"ALL CHANGE PLEASE ON PLATFORM 4," buzzed a deep, electric voice from the platform loudspeakers. "THE ELECTRO-TRAIN TERMINATES HERE. THIS IS THE FARMLANDS' TERMINUS. ALL CHANGE ON PLATFORM 4."

The metallic doors slid open, and Kate got down clutching her evening bag. Other passengers, like vague dabs, emerged from the neighbouring carriages, but she was more concerned in combatting her disillusion. Could this decrepit platform really be in the Southern Hemisphere? It looked more like a Western Hemisphere station she had seen while on a school outing a few years back, only this one was more rural and primitive. There was hardly any lighting, no clock, the seating was ancient and peeling, and desperate graffiti was scrawled everywhere. No romance here; but, she reflected, a station was only a station; no doubt the Farmlands would be very different.

The three labourers had also descended. While she hesitated, she heard them discussing whether to check in at a hotel first or go straight to the club. To her relief they decided on the latter and she was glad enough to follow them at a discreet distance behind.

Chapter Four

An hour later, Kate found herself standing outside the Rhythm & Blues nightclub, the three labourers having made their entrance a few moments earlier. The building's singular exterior excited her; its guitar-shaped door and brass trumpet roof; its windows spattered with staves and treble clefs, adorned with drifts of notes.

Unfastening her palla at the neck, she marched inside, her ears bombarded with the jazzy sound of brass instruments and hypnotic South African beat. There was a desk in the hall where she handed in her palla and paid her entrance fee. Then she advanced towards the swing doors at the far end.

She noticed that the doorman, a huge man in a check shirt, was scrutinizing her as she approached, and that his gaze was obviously unfriendly. This surprised her as, after all, she was only a young girl and posed no threat to himself or the nightclub. She strolled up to him confidently and presented her ticket with a smile. His frozen response was disconcerting; he seemed to be eyeing her clothes.

"You from the Eastern Hemisphere?" he asked at last.

"Yes." She remembered the black at the Electro-Terminus, who had reacted in a precisely similar fashion. Did they think that a girl could not take care of herself?

"Staying at a hotel overnight?"

"No," she told him. "I just came to the Farmlands to visit a nightclub, that's all."

The man frowned. "Alone?"

"Why not?"

He pursed his thin lips, searching her young face. "How old are you, Miss?"

"Eighteen", she lied, her eyes avoiding his stare.

"Hmmm."

"Look," she said, rather irritated by all this, "is there any reason why I shouldn't have come out here?"

The doorman shrugged and ripped the ticket in half, handing one half back to her. "None of my business, Miss," he said. "I'll let you in, but if there's any trouble, you're on your own. Don't expect me to come running. I've gotta take steps to cover myself, you understand."

Kate stuffed her half of the ticket into her evening bag. "I don't know what you mean," she said confusedly.

"Perhaps you'll find out before the night's up, Miss," he remarked sourly.

She turned away, finding his manner condescending and feeling slightly affronted by it. She had meant him no harm and considered herself to be a fairly decent person. She had her faults—who has not?—but she was no troublemaker, and to be accused before she had done anything was extremely offensive. For a split second, the painted face which had stared back at her so voluptuously from her bedroom mirror only a few hours before, turned ugly. But only for a second.

She pushed open the swing doors and entered a long room with a scattering of tables and a crescent-shaped stage at the far end. To the right stood the bar, a range of exotic-looking beverages hanging topsy-turvy against the wall above it. Directly beneath the bottles was a blackboard in the form of a guitar, with swirls of writing in violet chalk. It was all fascinating and new; even the names of the drinks were unknown to Kate, except the 'Mauve Liquor', and that she had never tasted.

"Hey, Miss, d'you want serving?" said the barman in front of her, in a jaunty, youthful voice.

"I'm not too sure what you've got, she replied, her eyes darting from his face to the blackboard.

"All on the board before you, Miss," he told her politely. "There's a 'Mauve Liquor', or a 'Mauve Heart' for them folks that prefer not to make themselves too intoxicated; a strong 'Double Bass' or milder 'Treble Clef' . . ." He picked up a cloth and began to wipe the bar. "Then there's a long, frothy 'Mauve Liquor' cocktail," he continued casually, "and our own speciality of the nightclub, a heady 'Rhythm & Blues.'"

Kate glanced towards the various drinks which had been ordered: a rich mauve liquid in a heart-shaped glass with its tall, slim stem spattered with minuscule, ultra-violet hearts; full litre beer mugs decorated with black double-basses, and frothy at the top tall octagonal glasses which looked nobbly and were filled to the brim with a liquid of deep ultramarine. But it was the broad, square-shaped glasses decorated with black semi-quavers which especially attracted Kate. They contained a lilac-coloured liquid with a generous head of pink froth, and two cocktail sticks—one with a guitar-shaped top and the other turned like a large treble clef.

"I'll have one of those, please," she said with a giggle. "They look fun."

"One Mauve Liquor cocktail comin' up," said the barman, pumping an empty, square-shaped glass a quarter full, and topping it up with a pink, soda-like fluid.

She paid him and took a tentative sip at the cool liquid, pasting her lips with foam. It was delicious, having a fruity, syrupy, creamy taste which was nothing like the Gold Liquor of her own quarter. Eagerly, she gulped several mouthfuls, then swung round on her stool to watch the band, feeling suddenly elated, as if the disappointments of the night were coming right after all.

Somebody else positioned themselves on an adjacent stool before the bar, and she heard the stranger say, in a light, Southern American accent: "A Mauve Liquor, please, brother."

As the barman went to serve, Kate turned back. By the accent she had expected the stranger's face to be a negroid one; but it was white, subtly tinted with a light, golden tan. His wistful, almond eyes were also golden. His nose turned up slightly at its tip; his light brown locks fell abundantly at his shoulders. She shifted her gaze to his frame, which was not exactly robust, but tall, slim and wiry. His check shirt was unbuttoned at the collar, exposing the upper part of his chest. His denim jeans were pale blue and tight fitting; their hems falling over black leather boots, neatly pointed at the toes.

As he drank, she noticed his long, slender fingers gripping the glass, like a musician's. The swaying of the liquid in the glass excited her, as did his tanned aesthetic face. She giggled again, deliberately drawing attention to herself. It did not occur to her for one moment that the physical attraction she felt for him might not be mutual. She knew that most young girls of her age had already found partners; why should she not do the same?

Rather than to her face, his eyes seemed drawn to her bright yellow stola and to the diamante bone pins which kept her long black hair in place. He took another sip from his glass.

"Are you from the Eastern Hemisphere, or is that just an Eastern Hemisphere outfit you're wearing?"

Kate was surprised that he should have noticed her costume, but she gave him a broad friendly smile. "Yes," she said. "As a matter of fact, I *am* from the Eastern Hemisphere."

"Gee." He ran a hand through his thick wavy hair. "You don't see many Eastern Hemisphere inhabitants around *these* spots. What's your name?"

"Kate Tiberius."

"Sounds like an Eastern Hemisphere name," he said, smiling wryly.

"How do you know that?" She looked at him with open curiosity.

"I was born in the Eastern Hemisphere of the United States," he explained, draining his glass. "I emigrated to the Southern Hemisphere with my folks when I was a kid; lived in the Synod ever since."

"You're a clergyman, then?" Kate gaped at him in surprise. His mellow laugh melted her insides.

"You're way out, honey," he told her. "My fate had already been mapped out for me when I lived in the Eastern Hemisphere. I'm a writer and musician. I do a lot of touring with my band; though when we do get the chance to do gigs at our home town in the States, there's nothing I enjoy more."

"Do you like it in the Synod?" she asked, subtly changing tack. "I mean, do you get on all right with the people there?"

"Aah—what the hell?" He shrugged. "At least its churches are pretty." He studied her empty glass. "How about another drink? My name's Guy, by the way."

"No thanks," she said regretfully, lowering her eyes. "I think I've already had too much."

"That's OK, honey. We all know when we've had about enough."

The barman drifted nearer, his eyes shining with awe, as Kate could not help but notice. The handsome young musician seemed to be held in high regard.

"You called, sir?"

"Yes, get me another Mauve Liquor. And buy a drink for yourself," said Guy, pulling a few crisp notes from his pocket and passing them over. He was sensual and cool in all his movements; Kate felt herself mildly attracted.

"It's funny," she mused aloud, as the barman went to fulfil the order, "how all the different classes and occupations are divided. It never used to be like that. At one time, you'd get an accountant and an athlete living in the same street. Well," she added pensively, "that's what I've been told, anyway."

He looked lazily in her direction, studying her—but, as she was bound to admit, in what seemed an offhand way. "Too many class riots, honey. And when it all came to a head sixty or seventy years ago, it was decided that we had to be segregated, or we'd tear each other to pieces. That's the only way it had to turn out, I guess. But there must have been some contention between the classes from the day jobs were invented. It wouldn't have blown up the way it did, otherwise."

But suddenly he seemed to lose all interest in the conversation, turning his head in the direction of the nightclub entrance. Someone had just come in and had taken all his attention. Kate twisted round and saw a tall, elegant quadroon woman wearing a glittery turquoise dress and sandals, who was gazing at him as fixedly as he stared at her. She was enchanting, Kate had to confess, with long, wavy hair that fell way below her shoulders. Despite her air of sophistication, she could not have more than twenty years of age. Kate had only to glance into Guy's almond eyes to realise the pull of real attraction.

"Hey, Emmaline!" he called out, pulling up an empty stool and beckoning to the quadroon girl. "Come here, honey." Kate could feel herself shrivelling inside as Emmaline strode confidently over to the bar. Placing herself on the stool Guy had reserved for her, she gave Kate a cool, appraising smile.

"Emmaline," said Guy, "meet Kate." Kate had to force herself to be polite; it was agony. "This is my girlfriend, Emmaline—born and bred in the Farmlands."

"Pleased to meet you, Kate." There was not a trace of hostility in Emmaline's eyes. But, as Kate reflected bitterly, there was no reason for any. She felt herself hopelessly outclassed. She was too young and too inexperienced to seek refuge in hate or vicious rivalry. She was only aware of acute intimidation; and when Guy put his arm around the quadroon girl, it was more than she could bear.

She stumbled from her stool like a frightened, helpless child. "I—I must go now," she stammered, frantically groping for her bag.

"Hey, Kate!" she heard Guy call after her as she began pushing through the blurry haze of bodies on the nightclub floor; but she did not turn her head. Only as she reached the swing doors did she pause for one last look at the Eastern Hemisphere native whom she had found so desirable. He seemed thrown off balance, which pleased her, but she felt slightly nauseated when, through the clamour of music and raised voices, she heard him say:

"Sorry, Kate—we meant no offence. It's just that you seemed so young."

The Electro-Trains stopped running at twelve-thirty in the morning. In the hall, having collected her palla, she glanced at her watch. It was just midnight. If she hurried, she should be just in time to catch the last one to the Eastern Hemisphere, then take a cab home. After her disappointing encounter with Guy, all she wanted was to get away.

The air outside, after the heated atmosphere of the club, was cool and soothing. On she went, retracing her steps along a narrow, winding path which led into an alleyway, where the darkness was as solid as a wall. The only light came filtering from the backroom of a sad-looking farmhouse nearby, which was crying out for a coat of paint. She had to hurry; time pressed. A sound of faint rustling from the bushes startled her ears.

She quickened her pace and was aware of another rhythm of footsteps not quite meshing with hers, which made her heart beat faster. She was finished with the Farmlands now; she had no desire to visit that section of the Southern Hemisphere again. She had suffered her dose of male rejection, from which all the paint on her face had not been able to protect her. The Eastern Hemisphere seemed like a world of light and understanding compared to this.

A sudden voice calling out behind her made her jump with fright.

"Oi, you!"

It's tone sounded harsh and abusive. She hurried from the alley without looking around, but to her alarm she found that she had not escaped.

"Oi, you!" repeated the voice in the same hostile tone. "Where do you think you're going?"

She wanted to flee, but her instincts told her that her pursuer might outrun her. Taking a long, deep breath, she decided to halt and turn round. He was a tall, heavily built young man whom she remembered having seen in the nightclub. She had not paid him much attention—Guy had engaged all that—but she had noticed, whenever she glanced in his direction, that he was staring fixedly at her in a resentful and disapproving manner. He opened his thick, rubbery lips to speak:

"I saw you in the nightclub. Why did you leave so early?" His accent had a Southern ring; probably it was typical of the native white inhabitants of the Farmlands section.

"I have to catch the last Electo-Train home," she replied.

He leant up against the wall, blocking her path. His hair, she noticed, was black and distinctly greasy, and brushed behind his ears. She began to be alarmed, and made an exaggerated show of examining her watch.

"I shall have to go at once if I want to catch my train. It's due in fifteen minutes."

"You can stop at my place for the night, can't you? I can see you to the station in the morning."

Innocent though she was, Kate understood what this would entail, and she reacted rather sharply, and perhaps unwisely.

"It's a pity Guy didn't offer me that," she simpered. "Well, I'm not interested if *he's* not interested—and as for any of the other men from the Farmlands, I'm not interested in *them*, either!"

The young man's porcine eyes danced like angry beads. "So, that's the way you choose to play it, is it? You shouldn't come out here, dressed like *that,* saying what you're saying." And with the flat of his large hand he pushed her up against the wall. "Anyone can see you're an Eastern Hemisphere inhabitant, and that you've poked your nose into a Southern Hemisphere nightclub; and you are under the legal age." Then he grabbed at her palla and tugged it.

The clasp of the brooch broke and the garment fell to the ground. Kate was terrified; she felt helpless and horribly exposed.

"How old are you—fourteen? Fifteen? It's a criminal offence for an Eastern Hemisphere inhabitant to go snooping around our nightclubs at that age. Didn't no-one ever tell you?"

She was trembling so much that the nod of her head went almost unnoticed. "Yes, but . . ."

"Well, your own quarter's going to do you for that," snapped the young man. "Do you good and proper."

She ducked her head under his outstretched arm in a desperate attempt to break free, merely worsening her predicament. He lunged at her, slapping her around the face with such force that she fell against the wall, bruising her back. The diamante bone pins slipped from her head so that a cloud of her hair was released to hang around her shoulders. Choking, her heart pounding with fear, she pulled herself up.

"Please," she whispered, breathing quickly and heavily. "Forgive me! I didn't mean what I said earlier. I wasn't thinking when I said it. Let me go—please!"

"The trouble with Guy," scowled the young man, viciously stabbing her in the collar bone with his forefinger "is that he's high on drugs.

He's in a world of his own. He's much too polite to tell people who don't belong—like you—where to get off!"

Tears trickled down her swollen cheeks; but no sound came from her lips.

"You stupid, mindless bitch!" You've done it all the wrong way round. Guy wouldn't waste his time on the likes of you, and you've gone and dug your own grave for him! If you think you'll be wearing a stola for much longer, you got another thing comin'. There's been cases of Eastern Hemisphere offenders like you before, and they end up in places far worse than the Farmlands!"

Then he punched her more seriously in the ribs several times. She was winded and collapsed, groaning, to the ground, her head coming forcefully into contact with the hard concrete pavement. After that he walked off and left her, crying and dishevelled, her left wrist covered in blood, her watch shattered in the dust by her side.

Chapter Five

The three labourers, swinging down the alleyway after their night out, came upon her half an hour later. Their solicitude was all that redeemed the worst evening of her life. They stopped a passing van and gently lifted Kate inside. At the nearest hospital, she received six stitches in her wrist, and was detained overnight. Thus it was not until Monday that she was able to catch her Electro-Train home. Fitzroy kindly accompanied her to the station and provided the money for her fare.

"Oh, dearie me," he said as he bade her farewell. "You was a sorry sight to see lyin' on de road in dat state; you really was. You should never have come out here, Miss. It could well have spoilt your good reputation."

"I see that now," she replied, "but surely no one need know where I went on Saturday night?" Her heart sank when she saw him shake his head.

"Them police patrols go snoopin', Miss," he told her. "They goes into them Farmlands' nightclubs lookin' for under age inhabitants from your quarter. I's seen it before. Sometimes they don't arrest them straight away, but come knocking on their doors once they's sure they's got the right person."

This reminded Kate of her attacker's malignant comments when he told her that she would be in deep trouble on her return to the Eastern Hemisphere. It had not occurred to her when she had set out so gaily on this adventure that it could lead to such fatal results.

Her mother, predictably, was horrified when she turned up at the villa looking like someone who had just walked into a wall. She insisted on a full explanation of Kate's disappearance and her behaviour; and Kate furnished one, knowing that there was no point in lying as she was bound to be found out sooner or later. Mrs Tiberius at once insisted that Kate report the incident to the police rather than waiting for the patrols to come visiting; a free and frank confession, she was sure, would mitigate the inevitable punishment to some degree. No one appeared to have any sympathy for Kate. What to her had seemed a piece of youthful exuberance, was to them evidence of a dangerous wilfulness of precisely the kind that was most feared.

Ten days later, she had the stitches removed from her wrist. Then in September, she was escorted to the Law Courts beside the Basilica, where she was brought to trial. Never in her worst dreams had she expected so dire a result as this. She remembered the shocked and forlorn expression on her mother's ashen face, as the judge announced that she was to be stripped of the family surname of Tiberius and that it would be replaced by the surname of the owner of her future place of abode. Further, that when she reached her sixteenth birthday, she was to be banished to the Non-Hemisphere quarter—a place of which she had heard the most lurid and horrifying stores—never to return.

Her mother's wail of protest was in vain. Then she too had burst into hysterical sobs, as a mass of unanswered questions bombarded her mind. What did it all mean? That she would never see Rebecca, or any other of her friends again? That she would be forced to give up her guitar lessons and her hope of becoming a musician, like Guy was? What about the rest of her education, so rudely cut short? Would she not be able to sit for her fifth year career examinations? It seemed that her whole life was to be blighted for one venial fault. And it awoke her indignation when she discovered that not the least effort was being made to bring her attacker to book.

An unhappy fortnight followed, during which her mother paid repeated visits to the Law Courts, returning each time with various documents. Kate assumed that her sentence was being worked out in detail, but she was as fearful of the subject as of an open wound, and shied away from discussing it. But one miserable evening in October, her mother called her to her room. She too was worried; Kate could see that she had lost weight.

"As you know, Kate," she said, "I have been paying regular visits to the Law Courts. I have been negotiating on your behalf, and arrangements have now been made as to who you are to live with after your departure from this quarter in December. God knows, I have tried to get them to show leniency, on the grounds that you have only recently lost your father, and that you may not have been quite yourself when you went to the Farmlands. But they know best; and the sentence stands."

"What about my schooling?" wailed Kate. "What about my career exams next May?"

"I shall visit your school tomorrow morning," replied Mrs Tiberius, keeping her eyes tightly shut, "to tell them that you will not be returning after the Christmas holiday. You will have reached the school leaving age by then."

"But unless I take my exams, I shall be leaving school without any qualifications!"

"The Law Court's decision was final," insisted her mother, sounding heartbroken. "I had no say in the matter. Do you think I like this predicament any more than you do?" It will hurt me, too, you know. I shall be horribly lonely after you've gone."

"I'm sorry, Mother," said Kate earnestly, "but I'm scared. I'm being sent to live the rest of my life in some place I don't even know; I feel that half of me is being cut away."

"Now, let's not get overwrought about this," said Mrs Tiberius, securing her hair with bone pins. "We're both distressed by what has happened, but we must try to be calm and sensible at such a time. I have many things to tell you; and I'd prefer to explain about them now, rather than leaving it all to the last minute."

Kate sniffed back her tears and said that she was listening.

"First, there's the question of where you should live. I have been in contact with your Aunt Nancy over the past fortnight. I think you met her once when you were little, at the Olympic Games. You may not remember her. Never mind. Nancy lives in her mother's former house, and has kindly agreed to take you in. She has no children of her own; her surname is Brannigan, which is the name you shall take. Apparently the house stands close to the north end of the Non-Hemisphere, in a close called 'Terminal Lane'. It's by the labyrinth, not far from the Northern Hemisphere where the white collar workers live and work. I think it would be best that you study to become a white collar worker in one of the Northern Hemisphere offices, which are not so far from your Non-Hemisphere abode. There are one and two-year secretarial courses at a college nearby. Your aunt has the address. She used to be a student there herself."

"What about my guitar lessons?" asked Kate, scowling down at the marbled floor of the villa. She looked up to see her mother sadly shaking her head.

"I know this will be hard for you to accept, Kate," said Mrs Tiberius, swallowing hard. "I know how much you wanted to be a musician; but it's just not possible now. Musicians don't live in the Non-Hemisphere—or the Northern Hemisphere for that matter; but at least you'll have a career."

"As a white-collar worker in the Northern Hemisphere, Mother?" interruped Kate caustically.

"As a white-collar worker in the Northern Hemisphere," agreed her mother resignedly. "But you never know; you might like it. I've lived in the Eastern Hemisphere all my life, so I've no idea what it will be like. But you've got to understand, Kate; you must train in something."

Kate felt angry and resentful. It was as if she had been dragged to the block and made to feel the edge of the axe of implacable fate. The villa fell silent for a moment except for the fountains which sang on unheard. She said: "When should I pack my things?"

"Oh, we can leave that for a while," replied her mother. She shot her daughter an uneasy glance. "Nancy tells me that you are not to wear a stola in the Non-Hemisphere, under any circumstances—and that goes for pallas and bone pins as well. I have sent her the money to buy you a range of Non-Hemisphere clothes, which she will send on to us via Electro-Mail. That will give you some idea of a suitable costume; but you're to leave all your stolas behind."

"Buy why, Mother?" asked Kate, shattered by this further blow.

"I think it has something to do with class bias", said Mrs Tiberius with a weary look. "You don't need me to tell you, of all people, of the tension that exists between the classes. There were terrible scenes years ago, which your grandmother witnessed when she was a girl; the authorities are not prepared to take any further risks. Nancy knows what she's talking about; you will do as she says."

"Why?" asked Kate reproachfully. "Is the Non-Hemisphere a dangerous place, then?"

"Any place or situation can prove dangerous if approached in the wrong way," came the sententious reply. "That's all I can say at this stage."

"All right, Mother," the girl agreed at last. "I promise I won't wear my stolas."

But as the day of departure grew closer, it was Kate who grew calmer, while Mrs Tiberius became more distraught. They parted finally with tears on both sides.

Chapter Six

The autumn sunlight filtering hazily through the curtains of the shabby bedroom in Terminal Lane brought Kate flickering back to consciousness. She stretched and got up from her bed, drawing back the curtains to gaze out at the familiar cul-de-sac with its horseshoe of thatched, dilapidated houses, and the sea massed turquoise beyond.

She heard her aunt's voice calling her from the passage. "Kate—get up now, will you? It's late enough. Come downstairs; you've got a letter from the Eastern Hemisphere.

Kate dragged on a dowdy green dress which lay over a chair and opened the door. Slowly, rubbing the sleep from her eyes, she made her way downstairs.

"Who's it from then?" asked Aunt Nancy with her usual curiosity, as Kate took the envelope from her, ripping it open at the top with her forefinger. Kate knew the identity of the writer before she had even unfolded the letter.

"It's from Rebecca," she replied.

Aunt Nancy still hovered. "I wonder what she's up to these days."

"She seems to be going along OK," said Kate tersely, skimming over the first two paragraphs. Then she read the remainder of the note:

> *"The main purpose of this letter is to inform you that I will not be a spinster for much longer. I am to be married to my fiance, Judah, in the spring of next year. I do hope you will be able to attend my wedding, the details of which I shall send you nearer the time. Judah and I have purchased a villa in Lancaster, which contains a small chapel and a long, covered veranda facing the garden.*
>
> *"We have agreed that I should carry on with my career as a commercial artist, but that once I'm married, I shall go freelance and work from home. Judah is to continue lecturing in Lancaster. I am determined not to give up my career, come what may, even when the time comes for me to have children. Judah fully supports me in this. It's the tradition amongst Eastern Hemisphere females, is it not, to learn how to defend ourselves physically, and to be independent in whatever career we pursue?*

*"Send Aunt Nancy my regards. I hope you are keeping well
and that you will be able to attend my wedding.*

"Kindest regards . . . Rebecca."

Kate moved towards the mirror which hung in the passage by the
front door. "Rebecca's getting married," she announced flatly.

"When?"

"Next May."

"About time, an' all."

"Why is it 'about time'?" asked Kate peevishly, uncomfortably
reflecting that Rebecca was five months younger than herself.

"Well, she'll be twenty-five by the date of the wedding, won't
she?" cried her aunt, glowering at her. "For a while I thought she'd
end up on the shelf, the way she kept on changin' 'er manfriends
an' changin' 'er mind as to whether or not she was going to settle
down."

Kate, standing before the mirror, was suddenly disconcerted by
the reflection that stared back at her from its mysterious depths.
Nine years had passed since the day of her trial, and she seemed
to be seeing herself for the first time. Her hair was still silky and
abundant, her porcelain skin soft and unlined, but Rebecca's letter

51

made her feel ugly and wretched and old. It was no credit to her that she should feel envious, when her only feeling should have been one of delight for her best friend; but she could not help it. And she hated what the mirror revealed and turned away sharply.

"What's up with you, Kate?" asked Aunt Nancy harshly. "You against marriage or somethin'?"

"For Heaven's sake, Aunt Nancy!" Kate cried, going into the lounge to collect her guitar which stood propped up against an alcove by the fireplace.

"Now where are you off to? Won't you be 'avin' any breakfast?"

"I don't want any breakfast," said the girl, grabbing her shawl and making for the front door. "I feel sick."

"You'd better watch yourself, Kate," warned her aunt, as her niece prepared to leave without another word. "You don't want all these petty things turnin' your mind."

Kate hurried towards the crooked curve of Terminal Lane's dead end. Slipping between its metal pillars, she descended the path leading to the golden shore beyond. Once on the sand, she took a few deep breaths and then flung herself down within a metre or so of a cluster of the ragged homeless, who sat there hopelessly, dulling their feelings by frequent recourse to the bottle.

How she howled inwardly at the pain which Rebecca's letter revived within her. For some reason, it brought back in all its dreadful details the attack she had suffered in the Farmlands on that evil summer morning nine years ago. Strangely, up until her late teens, she had managed to ride its horrors and seemed to be barely affected. For a few years she had still considered herself to be attractive, and had imagined that certain men would be bound to be drawn to her. She had fondly believed that she had cured herself. Not so; the lack of trust which had been planted then had grown insidiously. If ever a man were sharp with her, everything seemed to merge into one. The injustice of her own case still rankled; she was crippled, besides, with fear.

Her mind went back to Rebecca. To think they had practically grown up together, and were born in the same Eastern Hemisphere town! To think they had shared similar thoughts and ambitions; so many things they had once had in common! Now Rebecca's marriage would shatter that forever. Soon she would be leaving her parents' villa to live with a man and bear his children, happy and fulfilled. And Kate would be left mournfully behind like those poor vagrants, condemned to a half-life, to endless frustration!

The spasm subsided, as they often did, with an act of will. She stood upright, brushing off the sand and went with dragging steps back into Terminal Lane, securing her shawl tightly around her as the chill autumn wind howled and grew steadily fiercer.

An inn stood adjacent to the pillar of the cul-de-sac curve. It gloried in the name "The Three Blind Mice", and was a favourite resort for Non-Hemisphere inhabitants. Kate, fiddling with her guitar case, briefly surveyed the menu chalked on a board at the door, and ducked inside.

She was met at once with a potent odour of tobacco and Green Liquor and, as she found a table, her ears were assailed by the spiteful talk of a cluster of middle-aged spinsters at their usual game.

"My daughter 'ad an Eastern 'Emisphere maths tutor once," said one huge, red-faced woman, whose hips seemed a metre wide from where Kate was sitting. "'e was money-grabbin' an' all mouth, an' insulted everyone 'e came into contact with. 'E thought a lot of 'isself, he did, like all them well-to-do folk from the Eastern 'Emisphere." She took a sip of her drink, whilst her cronies waited patiently for the punchline. "Once 'e 'ad the nerve to turn up 'arf and hour late 'avin the cheek to fit another pupil in before me daughter's lesson."

"'Ard worker, was 'e?" remarked another. "Must of earned plenty of money, 'e must 'ave."

"Course 'e earned plenty o' money!" said the red-faced spinster tartly. "Earned it for 'is wife because 'e felt sorry for 'er, didn't 'e?"

"'Im what went round insultin' everyone, felt sorry for 'is *wife*? Don't give me that!"

"Oh yes," said the red-faced spinster. "A lovey-dovey little man 'e was about 'er, just after 'e suggested me daughter ought to be given a thick ear!"

"What did he say about 'er then?" asked several of the party of spinsters, sharpening the knives of their malice in anticipation.

"What did 'e say?" echoed the red-faced woman mockingly. "'e says to me all sorry-like: she don't drive and she don't work. She did go out to work just after leaving school, but she couldn't stand it no longer. Couldn't stand school no longer either, bless 'er little 'eart."

"Why's that, then?" asked one of the women. "Not all there, was she?"

"Aaah!" dismissed the red-faced spinster. "Smarter than the rest o' us put together, isn't she? She was an 'ousewife, so she stayed in the 'ouse, right? So the only thing she could do was 'ousework and she 'ad no children. Fact was," she continued, "I was beginnin' to feel sorry for 'er myself, until 'e told me they 'ad an 'oover at 'ome",

"So?"

"So," spluttered the large woman, "as well as not workin', she said she weren't strong enough to push the damn thing."

"So the damn thing was never pushed?"

"Course it was pushed!" said the woman, whose face looked as raw as a winter's morning. "'e pushed it, didn't 'e? And that's not the last of it. Before he left us for good, 'e knew me daughter 'ad learned nothin' from 'im; so this kind man who pushed the 'oover for 'is wife, turned the tables on 'er, sayin' she was the dimmest pupil 'e'd ever 'ad; and that a girl 'e' 'ad recently been teachin' Chemistry to got a grade two in 'er end o' year exam."

"Well," simpered another, "you know what answer *I'd* 'ave given 'im: per'aps if you'd spent less time pushin' the 'oover for yer wife, she'd 'ave got a grade one!" At which point the whole party of women fell about laughing.

Defeatest talk of a more subdued kind was coming from a table to Kate's right. There, two shabbily dressed young Non-Hemisphere men were sitting with mugs of 'Sea Jade' before them, the quarter's equivalent to beer.

"You signed on yet?" asked one of them, his mouth plugged with a cigarette of an inferior brand.

"Tuesday," mumbled the other. "I could do with some cash. I need to feed the meter to 'eat me lodgings. Can't afford to get ill with the NHS in the state it's in."

"I sign on next Thursday," said the first, removing the cigarette from his lips. "Bloody walk to the dole office, you know," he added in a discontented tone. "I 'ave to troop right down 'Crofter's Road', past the Electro-Terminus." He paused to drain his glass; then he set it down firmly. "I 'ate that bleedin' Electro-Terminus. It reminds me of all the jobs I ain't got. Every time I pass it to sign on, I see all them 'Emisphere bods on their way to work in this quarter, wearing their macs so they don't look conspicuous; but you can tell a mile off that they ain't one of us."

"Yeah," said the other with relish. "But they got to wear 'em, in't they? I remember one of them coming down here without his mac, oh so nice, oh so fine."

"What 'appened to 'im, then?"

"Silly sod got his head kicked in, di'nt 'e? Serve the stupid bastard right! They think they can shame us, wearing the toga. Soon deal with 'em!"

"Yeah! Their 'Emisphere women need a good beltin' an' all!" shouted the red-faced spinster who had been listening in on the two men's conversation. "What d'you say, fellas?"

"They *all* need a good beltin'," said the first man with finality. "Each an' every one of them."

Kate could stand no more of this. She got up and went to the bar. A barmaid whom she had not seen before came forward at once to serve her and she was like a light in a dark place. She was young and beautiful, with a smooth, unwrinkled skin and eyes the colour of emeralds. Her long chestnut hair fell abundantly below her shoulders. Her delicate lips were like cherries; her figure was shapely and petite. Everything about her projected an aura of youth and vitality; an innocent freshness that Kate had long since lost.

"Oh, Christ!" said the girl, in a vivacious, proletarian accent, looking from the spinsters to the two men at the table. "How they rabbit on! Sometimes I think that's all they come in 'ere for, to grumble!"

"I don't come in often myself," said Kate, with a polite, reserved smile.

"What are you 'avin' then?" the barmaid asked boldly. "A Green Liquor do you?"

"Yes, that would be fine," said Kate, as she marvelled at the girl's peach-like beauty.

The drink was expertly poured and placed on the bar. Kate produced her money. It was then that the girl noticed the guitar case.

"You play that?"

"Yes, I do," replied Kate, "though not so much nowadays."

"Fancy playin' in 'ere, then?"

"Well, I . . ."

"Hang on a minute," said the barmaid impetuously, moving from the bar. "I'll go an' ask the landlord about it."

"No, wait!" called Kate after her, for she hated to be rushed into any decision. "I think that, after all, I . . ."

Kate frowned and looked around the room. The spinsters still sat hunched in their chattering group. Other visitors came and left, pushing through the haze of tobacco smoke. Everything was tarnished, stained, grotty. There was no future for her here, and she turned unobtrusively to make her exit. But a voice at her elbow stopped her. The man said:

"Kathy here tells me that you're going to give us a song this morning."

It was the landlord, with the girl standing earnestly by his side. Kate stared into his narrow brown eyes.

"Well, I . . ."

"Go on, Miss," said several people by the bar. "Don't be shy! Give us a song!"

Kate addressed the landlord. "Do you mind self-compositions?" she asked timidly. "It's all I know."

"Whatever you've got to offer us, love," he replied with a grin.

Kate would have been glad of any excuse to get away, and keep her lips sealed; but the clamour for her music had been taken up by the customers all along the bar, and she knew she could not back out now with a good grace. It was strange; all her life she had wanted to be a musician, and yet when the opportunity to perform came, she was almost crushed with self-doubt.

She gripped her guitar and mounted the small platform at the rear of the inn. Everyone gathered round to listen, and while Kate hastily removed her guitar from its case, she announced what she was going to sing. It was a ballad called "The Down And Outs"; she had composed it shortly after her departure from the Eastern Hemisphere and it summed up for her all the sharp uncertainty she had suffered at that time.

The talk in the room suddenly died, and it became very still. A more attractive audience she could not have wished for. But as her fingers moved to find the first chord, Kate forgot all about them and their curious faces. She was wrapped in the emotions which her playing and her voice conveyed:

> *"All gone. I can't see what surrounds me. I've been turned away from the place I know. Down and Outs are the ones who have found me. But I can't adapt, so where can I go?"*

She sang the chorus and the second verse with growing confidence as she realised how well they were being received.

"Well, they're getting more than their fair share. Whilst you're not getting you share at all. And you're looked at as if you're not there. And you can't find a mentor to call."

"Nearly broken. Well, we all have our problems. I scowl with a pain that they'll never know. Well, they're getting more than their fair share. While you're not getting your share at all . . ."

As she strummed the last chord, the room erupted with applause. She found herself smiling in exultation, and as she descended from the stage she was met by the landlord, with Kathy following close behind.

"That was absolutely fantastic, love!"

"I told you so, didn't I, Mr Allinson?" put in Kathy brightly. "I told you she'd be of some 'elp to us."

"Help to you?" asked Kate, confusedly. "How on earth could I be of help to you?"

"Simple, love," replied the landlord, pressing a crisp note into her palm at which she stared in amazement. "As a matter of fact, our reg'lar Saturday mornin' singer 'as just jacked in the job, and we was lookin' for somebody to replace 'im. Both Kathy and myself agree that you'd do just fine, eh, Kathy?"

"Yeah," said the girl, her emerald eyes twinkling with delight.

"So, what do you say to that?"

"I'd be honoured," said Kate, stuffing the note into the pocket of her guitar case in excited agitation. "When can I start?"

"Come next Saturday—nine o'clock sharp."

"All right," said Kate, as she threaded her way towards the swing doors. "Yes, I will. And thank you!" she added, before the darkness swallowed her up. "Thank you so very much!"

Chapter Seven

Kate was reading a letter which she had just received from her mother in the Eastern Hemisphere.

> *"I write as the weather grown steadily colder, reminding me that it will soon be your birthday. I find it hard to believe that you will be twenty-five this December. Time flies by so quickly. It seems like only yesterday that you were a toddler, a metre high, running about like a mad thing in bare feet, and your hair tied back in plaits.*

> *"No doubt Rebecca has informed you that she and Judah are to be married next May. It is such wonderful news. I am so pleased for them both. I realise how close to two of you were, and how happy for her you must be . . . ."*

Kate rested the letter temporarily on the table, letting out her breath in a sharp sigh. Every one of her mother's kindly meant words seemed to cut her like a knife. She shook her head and brought her eyes back to the page:

"In the letters that you write to me, you sound rather lonely and unoccupied; or is there something in your life that you are not keeping me informed about? Thinking about Rebecca's wedding makes me wonder whether you, yourself, have yet found a partner. I know things were made difficult for you in that respect after that unfortunate attack inflicted upon you nearly ten years ago; but it's just a thought.

"You did very well to achieve the mauve belt in Karate shortly after your arrival in the Non-Hemisphere; I was most impressed! To think that, at one time, you knew no self-defence at all! You excelled in your secretarial examinations also; I am only sorry that a career in the Northern Hemisphere offices did not work out for you. I hear that Aunt Nancy suffered the same disappointment; but if you are both happy, that is all that matters. I long for you to be happy; I'm sure that's what your father would have wanted, too. He always hoped you would settle down in a life of your own, with many friends; but I'm sure that the time will come soon. It's not too late; you're still young.

"The main purpose of this letter is to ask you about your plans for Christmas, as we are already well into October and the festive season will soon be upon us. I am aware that you are restricted to not more than seven days in the Eastern

Hemisphere each year; but as you have not used up any of your allocation so far this year, perhaps you would care to spend a full week at the villa over Christmas? It would be lovely to see you again for that length of time. Please write and confirm either way. I shall try to arrange for Rebecca to come over Christmas Day. I do hope you will be able to attend her wedding next spring."

"Send my regards to Aunt Nancy. I hope you are both keeping well.

"Write soon. Fondest wishes . . . Mother."

Folding the letter into a square, Kate placed it in a box in her dressing table drawer. She would wait a fortnight before replying. She would respond to Rebecca's letter at a later date.

She went downstairs into the lounge to collect her dole card from the rack on the mantelpiece where all loose papers were indiscriminately pushed in. It was Tuesday morning; time for her to keep her regular fortnightly appointment at her local dole office. By a cruel mischance, one of Rebecca's letters had accidentally become paper-clipped to her dole card; she shook it away as she bitterly reflected on Rebecca's life in relation to her own. How they had diverged! As for herself, she now had no home. She remembered being taught Religious Knowledge at her school in the Eastern Hemisphere; the Non-Hemisphere had always reminded her of limbo.

As she opened the front door, she listened for Aunt Nancy, who was presumably still asleep; all was quiet in that sad and shabby house. The mirror was to her right but she shunned her reflected self, as she tended to do nowadays. In happier days long ago, she would have never ventured outside without first glancing in the glass in youthful anticipation.

An icy hail was falling. Wrapping her shawl tightly about her, she trudged up Terminal Lane. Her umbrella would have afforded her some protection, but her thoughts had been so distracted as she had set out that she had come without it. She was still not far from the house, but she decided against returning for it for fear of waking her aunt. She did not want to have to communicate with her; these days they seemed to have little in common.

Still, she thought, turning down the path that led to the shore, she could find refuge from the elements in the labyrinth; one branch of this began among the rocks at the end of the beach. On she tramped, cursing this vile weather, and vaguely registering the lighthouse whose throbbing light further out guided the ships to safety. Then she paused, raising her hand to test the air, and found that the hail had stopped.

The sky was still gloomy overhead. Birds moved heavily across it—crows, she thought. The sun was a lustreless globe, veiled. She stood close by the entrance to the labyrinth and peered in, remembering as she did so, the misery of her daily trek to work six years ago. It was a mere twelve minutes' walk through this stone tunnel to her office, if you ascended by its stuffy, claustrophobic lift; slightly longer by the steps. By choice, she would have spent all her days walking, that she might have been spared the torture of working amongst the cannibals of the dreadful office jungle. How glad she would have been if she had never arrived at all!

Hearing the rhythmic patter of footsteps, she looked up, startled, in time to see a man in a red mac hurriedly making his way into the complex. From the case he carried, she would have judged him to be a businessman, but a wave of exhilarated unease shot through her as she noticed his swift athletic stride. His shoulders were straight; his head was held high, his expression utterly fearless. He moved like a sportsman from the East.

There was no one else about. The sky was once more in turmoil, threatening a fresh assault. The man gracefully descended the narrow steps before her, and she found herself following, both to seek refuge and to pursue him. He never looked back and she was afraid that she would never catch up with him, though she quickened her pace. But she knew that unless she did, the yearning that was already nagging at her insides would grow worse. Somehow she felt as if she were a part of him, as, for the first time in many years, she found herself experiencing the cravings of lust.

A squally breeze driven by the confused weather systems down the tunnel, dragged her shawl briskly from her, and pressed in against the grey stone wall, as if it too were in the grip of its own inanimate passion. Flustered, she pulled it back, pealing it off the wall as the man continued on his way. His figure was diminishing before her; he marched ahead like a herald at the Games.

Then suddenly he was passing the neon arrow indicating the way to the dangerous sophistication of the Northern Hemisphere quarter, and she too was emerging into a large, built-up area which she knew well. This was "New City Road", where the traffic habitually clogged the street and the pavements jostled with pedestrians both servile and aggressive according to status. To her left stood the unlovely office block where she had toiled as a shorthand / typist until her disgust and her dismissal had worked together to remove her from that environment. To its immediate right stood the exploitative "Nine to Five" employment agency, which had introduced her to the wretched firm. The adjoining estate agents gave way to a jeweller's shop and a bank, beyond which rose an inn called "The Capital"; and it was into this that the businessman swiftly disappeared. Apprehensive, yet undeterred despite her incongruous Non-Hemisphere attire, she took a deep breath and followed him inside.

The interior was so different from those of the inns in her own quarter that it made her catch her breath. No atmosphere of fug here, of defeat scarcely held at bay! The seats were of a plush velvet and ran neatly around the walls; the cushions were tassled and luxurious. Confident men and women sat at the tables; their deferential inferiors subtly kept their place. The contrast for Kate was all the greater in that she did not remember having ever set foot inside a Northern Hemisphere inn during her short-lived days as a white-collar worker. She had not been invited, and had not dared to go alone. Disillusion made her bolder now.

She had hoped that the man she had been following would be alone, but she saw him talking to another businessman at the bar, his red mac now folded neatly over his arm. Both men were drinking Red Liquor, the traditional drink of this quarter, which Kate had often seen but never tasted. Her body tensed up as she saw the other man drain his glass and swagger out of the inn.

She braced herself and strolled forward, to lean with both elbows on the bar. She realised that this was an immature gesture designed to attract attention, but she could not help herself; she was lonely, and jobless, and generally bored with life. She fiddled with her shawl, pulling and stretching it until its fringes brushed the sleeve of his jacket. That made him turn; she detected a hint of irritation in his azure, deep-set eyes.

"Sorry," he sighed, his voice deep and masculine. "Am I in your way?"

"My fault," she answered meekly. "I should have realised I was brushing your jacket with my shawl. I ought to be more careful, I suppose."

"Mmm," he remarked, noticing her costume with disapproval, "perhaps you should, though you're leaving it a bit late. It's obvious to me that you're not from the Northern Hemisphere. Whatever possessed you to come into a Northern Hemisphere inn?"

"Who knows?" she answered him sarcastically. "Perhaps I just felt like it. I'm sick of all this class-conscious trash. Besides," she added, peering at him, "I'm not convinced that you originate from this quarter either. You don't look much like a Northern Hemisphere inhabitant to me."

His censorious expression changed to one of mild astonishment. "How can you tell? What knowledge do you have of the Hemispheres?"

This 'placing' of her was humiliating; though she had to acknowledge to herself that it was inevitable. She replied bitterly: "It's a long story. I hate going into it at the best of times. But you," she continued, staring deeply into his eyes, "I am sure you're from the Eastern Hemisphere. Your hair's not too short, and your movements are rather athletic. I'm right, aren't I?"

"Well, yes," he replied. "I did come from there originally, but now I live permanently in the Northern Hemisphere." He fumbled in his pocket for his wallet. "Look, can I offer you a drink?"

"No," she said, almost defensively, "I think I'll get one myself."

He seemed surprised, but she boldly ordered Red Liquor from the barman. On receiving the beverage, she held it up to the light. It swirled around in the glass; rich, thick and bloody. Smiling mischieviously, she brought it to her lips and swallowed a rash, huge mouthful, choking on it instantly till her eyes streamed with tears. She had never tasted anything so repulsive. She pushed the glass aside, still coughing.

"I don't know how you can drink that stuff," she groaned to her companion, who was watching her with amusement. "It's vile!"

"It's an acquired taste," he told her.

She wiped the tears from her face and settled herself. "So, you've lived in the Northern Hemisphere for some time?"

"Seven years," he replied, "ever since I was twenty-three. I used to be an athlete in the Eastern Hemisphere, and regularly took part in the International Olympics. My specialist area was biathlon, but I trained in martial arts as well."

"Oh, which ones?" asked Kate, her ears pricking up.

"Green belt Aikido; Green belt Judo; Brown belt Karate."

"That's fantastic!" she exclaimed.

"That's the Eastern Hemisphere," he replied proudly.

She lowered her gaze to the inn's carpeted floor, musing on her own missed opportunities.

"Yes," he continued, lifting the medal that he wore around his neck, "this is the gold I won in the biathlon competition in the Olympics eight years ago. I still ski, actually," he added. "My wife, Marjatta, comes from the Eastern Hemisphere in Finland. We go skiing there twice a year with Lenni, our four-year-old daughter."

"Oh, I see," murmered Kate, absorbing this piece of unwelcome information.

Tactfully, he changed the subject. "My name's Bruce, by the way. What's yours?"

"Kate. Nice to meet you, Bruce." Then their eyes met and, for all her embarrassment, she could see that the attraction was mutual.

Shall we go for a walk?" she said, trying to maintain an air of casualness.

"Oh, I'm afraid not," he sighed, checking his watch. "I've to report to the office in a few minutes, after which I have to travel to Shaftesbury to see a client. I'm an insurance representative," he added, "in case you haven't already gathered. But we must see each other again—very soon."

They both rose together and threaded their way through the tables to the exit, where they halted outside the jeweller's shop and within the shadow of a large, dome-shaped museum.

"I must leave you now," he said, placing an earnest hand upon her shoulder. "Meet me outside the labyrinth beside New City Road at eleven o'clock on Sunday morning."

"I'll be there," she breathed warmly.

"Until then," he said, moving swiftly away.

"Until then," she echoed happily. And the next moment he had disappeared from sight.

Chapter Eight

A mist like a fine fume drifted from the sea, filling the autumnal air with a fragrance of its own. Waves lapsed on the beach, splashing quietly; the spots of water on Kate's shoes shone like jewels.

"It's going to be a beautiful day," she said to herself as she strolled along.

"Yes, a beautiful day!" echoed a young voice close at hand. Kate stopped in surprise and turned towards the rock where a girl was standing and smiling, her chestnut hair just lifted by the wind. The lighthouse sent its strobe towards the horizon, where the sun was struggling to rise.

"Kathy!" she cried in delight.

"Yeah, that's right. Fancy seen' you here! You remember my name, then?" said the cheerful girl.

"But of course!" said Kate, with a warm smile. "I have reason to be grateful. You found me that job at the Three Blind Mice."

"And why not?" shrugged the other. "You're a bleedin' good performer. What's your name, by the way?"

"Kate."

They moved on slowly together, keeping parallel with the front of tiny waves. Kathy jerked her beautiful head in the direction of the lighthouse.

"They say that light'ouse is 'aunted," she commented. "Never been inside it meself, mind." Abruptly she turned to face Kate, studying her with her large, emerald eyes. "You're quite well spoken, aren't you? Do you come from around 'ere then?"

"No," answered Kate wearily. "I'm from the Eastern Hemisphere."

"Cor, really? The Eastern Hemisphere? Well, for Gawd's sake! What on earth did you want to come 'ere for?"

"I didn't want to," Kate replied softly, scratching at the sand with her toe. "I was sent here as a punishment."

"Oh? What did you do?" asked Kathy, who clearly had never dreamt of such a thing.

"I went to a Farmlands' nightclub when I was under age. That's a criminal offence in the Eastern Hemisphere, you know. The awful thing about it is," she continued, revealing the scar on her wrist, "that on my way back to the terminus, I was attacked by this beast of a man in an alleyway."

Kathy stared at her, but now, it seemed, with sympathy and understanding. "What, sexually?" she asked.

"Oh no."

"*I* was," Kathy told her almost truculently. "I was bleedin' raped outside an inn when I was thirteen. Luckily I didn't get pregnant; but it was bloody painful at the time."

"What did your mother and father say?"

"Me dad was dead, weren't 'e?" replied Kathy, fiddling with her long chestnut hair. "As for me mum—well, you know what it's like. They don't feel as protective towards their daughters as fathers do, do they?"

"I suppose not." Kate studied her friend's pure, unblemished face. "How old are you, Kathy?"

"Seventeen, the middle of next month," replied the girl with a sigh. "Soon comes round, don't it? All right, I was hurt," she continued defiantly, "but I'm determined to make somethin' of my life. I can read an' write, you know, an' I'm goin' to put that to use. Me mum and dad could read an' write, an' all. They taught me when they could. I'm proud of that, I am."

"That's very commendable in this quarter," remarked Kate. She was watching the powerful lighthouse beam rebutting the mist. "Do you mean you've taken up writing to make use of that knowledge?"

"Oh, good Lord, no!" laughed Kathy. "I'm not as good as all that! No, I won't be workin' at the Three Blind Mice no longer on Saturdays after mid-January. I've only been puttin' in time there to scrape enough money for a three-month shorthand / typist's course I started in September. They let me into college on the basis that I can read 'an write, see? An' when I finish in January, I can work as a white-collar worker in the Northern 'Emisphere—somethin' I've always wanted to do. Why, what's the matter?" she added, seeing Kate's frowning expression. "Does the thought of that make you sick or somethin'?"

Kate sighed. "That's what you've made up your mind to do, is it?"

"Look," retorted Kathy belligerently, "if you don't like the sound of it, just say so straight out. I want to better myself—to do somethin' with me life. Surely that's not so difficult to understand?"

"What does your mother think about it?"

"Oh, me mum!" exclaimed Kathy, with a bright smile. "She's all for it. She used to be a shorthand / typist in the Northern 'Emisphere 'erself, only things didn't work out for 'er."

"No, I can imagine."

"Just because she was unlucky, doesn't mean the same thing will 'appen to me, does it?" insisted the girl truculently. "Why the 'ell should it? We're two different people, aren't we? Anyway, even though it didn't work out for 'er, she's still keen for me to go ahead. Any more objections?"

Kate remained silent, not wishing the subject to develop into an argument. She thought of the deviousness of the older generation in encouraging their daughters into employment in a cruel, cut-throat world where they could never hope to achieve a permanent position. Why didn't people who had the experience tell the truth?

"I want to earn a livin'," continued Kathy, the amicable expression returning to her face. "I want money in me purse to do what I want with. Me mum 'asn't 'ad a new coat in fifteen years. I want to be in a position to get 'er one. And when I get that job," she added with determination, "I'm goin' to get a small place of me own instead of stayin' cooped up at 'ome till me mother dies an' leaves me the 'ouse. Oh, Kate! I can't wait till January! I can't wait to be workin' in that posh Northern 'Emisphere quarter with freedom to come and go as I please! It's goin' to be fantastic!" She stared down suddenly with a delighted expression. "Hey, look! The water's so still I can see me own reflection!"

Kate stooped to catch sight of her own, but the unsteadiness of her companion soon disturbed her attention. Kathy's cheeks looked pale; she caught her arm firmly and led her to sit on the rocks.

"What's the matter?" she asked her. "I thought you were going to faint. Here, take some deep breaths and get the colour back in your cheeks. Are you eating properly?"

"I'm on a diet", explained the younger girl. She sat down without demur. "I've 'ad nothin' to eat since lunchtime yesterday."

"You don't need to diet, Kathy!" exclaimed Kate incredulously. "You're gorgeously slim as it is."

"Yes, and I want to remain slim, don't I?" said the other with a fierce look. "Bloody marvellous, isn't it? I'm nearly seventeen years old, an' I've still never 'ad a boyfriend. Disgraceful, ain't it? It's as if I'm not normal or somethin'."

"So, that's why you're dieting?"

"Well—obviously. I wouldn't do it for the sheer 'ell of it, would I?"

Kate felt a stab of pain as she thought of the men this lovely girl would soon be working with in the offices of the Northern

Hemisphere. So young and bright-eyed; how could she disabuse her of her hopes? And she was a little dazzled herself by the overflow of the other's innocence and optimism. Perhaps history did not always repeat itself. Perhaps, just this once, one bold spirit could break the pattern?"

"Come along,?" she said, getting to her feet. "Not eating in twenty-four hours is not good enough. You need looking after. Come back to my place and meet my aunt."

Chapter Nine

"I have a confession to make," Kate said to Bruce, as they strolled arm in arm down New City Road. "I was reluctant to tell you on our first meeting in case it might scare you away."

"I'm made of tougher material than you might imagine, Kate," he told her firmly; and, reassured by his confidence, she went on.

"Do you remember, almost as soon as we met, how I worked out that you weren't from the Northern Hemisphere?"

"What of it?"

"The fact is, I could tell you were from the Eastern Hemisphere merely by seeing you walk down the road. That's what attracted me to you in the first place."

They turned into Politician's Square and entered one of the fashionable restaurants there, to have lunch. There were distractions and interruptions—wine to order, the menu to peruse. When finally, they had sent the waitress away, Bruce turned to her again.

"You were saying?"

"Oh yes, my great confession. What I really meant to tell you was that I too was born in the Eastern Hemisphere."

"Good Heavens!" He put down his glass and stared at her in surprise. "I thought you sounded rather well-spoken for an inhabitant of the Non-Hemisphere. So, how on earth did you end up living in that quarter?"

"Can't you guess?" she said.

"You did something wrong?"

"I'm afraid so."

"What, seriously?"

She nodded, shamefaced. "I went to a Farmlands nightclub before I was sixteen."

"That *is* serious," said Bruce solemnly. "What on earth possessed you to do that? Weren't you warned of the hazards?"

"My father had just gone for a soldier and been killed," she explained. "I suppose I went a bit haywire afterwards. I was confused. I needed guidance." She sighed. "Anyway, they sent me to the Non-Hemisphere before I had a chance to finish schooling. I wanted to be a musician, but of course my hopes were ruined. So I trained to be a white collar worker; but I had only been working for a short spell in a Northern Hemisphere office when I found myself unemployable; blacklisted."

"All white collar workers from the Non-Hemisphere *are* blacklisted," said Bruce, nodding his head. "They drift in and out of the firm I work for all the time. None of them have been kept on for more than six months. It's nothing to take personally. It's a policy to keep the classes segregated. Which in your case," he added, raising his glass again, "doesn't seem to have worked."

"Entering that pub to meet you, you mean? Well, I don't see why I shouldn't. I'm not going to kowtow to these ridiculous restrictions."

"You've already seen what they can do if you don't, Kate," Bruce warned her. "It's a class-conscious world; you can't alter the facts. Those riots at the beginning of the century were pretty horrendous from what I've heard. The whole of society had to be restructured from top to bottom. And it works, in a fashion, you have to confess; though the rules have to be artificially maintained. Trying to rebel against them could cost you your life. When I left the Eastern Hemisphere, I didn't come over to the Northern Hemisphere quarter in a toga."

"Why *did* you come over?" she asked him, curiously. "You sounded to have been successful where you were. It seems a pity to throw it all up to sell insurance."

"That may be the way *you* see it, Kate," he replied, getting on his dignity a little. "But my viewpoint is different."

"How do you mean?"

"My dear Kate, you make no secret of your hostility to the ethos of the Northern Hemisphere. It may surprise you perhaps to learn that I found the pressure and competition of being an Eastern Hemisphere athlete far worse. When success comes easily, you're in clover; but if by any chance you fail to win a medal—which is inevitable, after all—your manager is only too ready to drum you out of the sport."

"Really?" Kate was surprised.

"You have my honest word. Of course, losing my occupation as an athlete would not have been the end of the world," he continued. "I could have always become a coach, if the worst had come to the worst. No, I left the Eastern Hemisphere for another reason."

"What was that?"

"Quite honestly, I abandoned it because its customs and way of life did not appeal to me. My wife is in total agreement, and we certainly would not want Lenni to grow up in that sort of environment."

"I can't understand that," said Kate, shaking her head in disbelief. "Anyway, is that fair to her, just because you and your wife didn't like it?"

"If Lenni cuts her teeth on Northern Hemisphere ways," persisted Bruce, convinced that he was right, "then she'll grow up not knowing any differently. We've still taught her to ski, and in a few years' time, when she's mature enough, we'll instruct her in the arts of self-defence and shooting. These are all Eastern Hemisphere customs, and we approve of them; but that's as far as we shall take it."

He searched her face, expecting her to protest. When she remained silent, he went on:

"Actually, it surprises me that you remain loyal to the Eastern Hemisphere after what they've done to you. After all, they've robbed you of your qualifications and prospects; taken you away from your friends and cast you out to live among the down and outs of society. How often are you allowed back there to see your family—one week out of fifty-two? Isn't that just adding a further sting to the punishment? They show you what you've been removed from and then they snatch it away again. That's cruelty in my eyes. I'm sure you cannot disagree with me on that count."

"No," said Kate, "I don't disagree with you there. But, you see, the idea of becoming a musician has always appealed to me, and it's in the Eastern Hemisphere where musicians are trained. I couldn't stand working in an office; I wouldn't go back to it even if I were given the chance. Besides," she muttered, suddenly embarrassed, "there was more to my punishment by the Eastern Hemisphere Law Courts than that."

He noticed her awkwardness and asked her tentatively what more there was. And so, taking courage, she began to tell him of the abuse she had received at the hands of the drunken Farmlands' man, and how the experience had continued to affect her. It was not something she had discussed with a man before.

"I was really stupid," she went on, having made this further confession. "I had all those opportunities in the Eastern Hemisphere to learn self-defence as a child—my father kept urging me. If only I had had the sense! I think you're quite right to make sure that Lenni is taught. It's a violent world out there."

"She will attend classes," said Bruce resolutely, "but we can always help her to practice between times. My wife has a mauve belt in Karate.

"So have I," retorted Kate, immediately resenting the fact that his wife should have reached the same stage as herself in an activity they had both happened to pursue. "I took Shotokan Karate lessons as soon as I came over to the Non-Hemisphere," she went on proudly. "In the Eastern Hemisphere I did archery. We set up targets in our garden and practised shooting on Sundays. I used to enjoy archery." Her voice became wistful as she remembered. "I didn't bring my bow and arrows with me, though, because in the Non-Hemisphere I knew there would be nowhere to practice."

"You obviously have an interest in sport," said Bruce. "I must take you to the International Olympics next March."

"Yes," she said, and her eyes began to shine again. "That would be nice."

Chapter Ten

Kate was writing to her mother. Beyond her window the sea twinkled and danced, but she felt drained of all vitality. Her pen dragged and often hovered over the page. She began:

"Dear Mother, I write to you on a cold Sunday morning in November, reflecting as I do so that though my heart is always with you, we now stand physically light years apart.

"Rebecca has indeed informed me about her wedding, although she has not yet confirmed the exact date on which it is to be held. I am delighted for her and hope that she and Judah have a long and happy life together.

"In your last letter to me, you mentioned about jobs, friends and a partner. I am sure it will please you to hear that I have at last found a friend. Her name is Kathy; she has a Saturday job as a barmaid at an inn near here. Oh, Mother, I wish you

could meet her. She is one of the most beautiful young women I have ever seen. Her skin is like ivory, smooth and milky white; she has green sparkling eyes and long chestnut hair. Do I sound envious? Well, perhaps I am. She found me a job at the inn as a singer and guitarist; isn't that marvellous? You know how I have always wanted to be a musician. It gives me the chance to perform some of the songs I composed in my teens, and others that I have written since coming to the Non-Hemisphere, which you have never heard.

"Now I have some pleasing news on the subject of partners. I have actually managed to find one. His name is Bruce, and he works in the Northern Hemisphere as an insurance representative. Oddly enough, he was originally from the Eastern Hemisphere; I suppose that's why I like his company. I've only been out with him a few times, as I only met him last month, but I'm sure our relationship will develop in time. He has promised to take me to the International Olympics at the end of March. So there you are; that's three of your wishes come true in one letter."

She paused, sighing deeply, and stared out of the window. Tears had started to her eyes. Frowning, she blinked them away and concentrated once more on her writing:

"Yes, Christmas will indeed be upon us very soon; in less than two months, in fact. I am sorry; you must think me

very neglectful not having come to see you at all throughout this year. I appreciate that it would not be fitting for Rebecca or yourself to set foot in the Non-Hemisphere quarter, but it occurs to me that perhaps we could all meet up for the International Olympics next March. I shall mention it to Rebecca when I next write to her.

"As for Christmas, I'm sure Rebecca would rather spend it at home with her parents than with myself. Don't forget, this will be her last Christmas as an unmarried daughter, and that is something I'm sure even Judah would allow for and appreciate.

"Now for my own plans. I have decided to take the ten o'clock Electro-Train from the nearest Electro-Terminus on the morning of Christmas Eve. It should reach the Eastern Hemisphere Terminus by approximately ten fifty-five that same morning. I will stay overnight at the villa, and return to the Non-Hemisphere on Boxing Day morning. Please write soon and confirm if you are in agreement with this.

"Give my regards to your new neighbour, Deborah. You often mention her in your letters; I'm glad you get on so well with her. As always, I send my fondest love to yourself. Tell Rebecca I will be writing shortly.

"Write soon . . . Kate."

She re-read what she had written and shoved it in an envelope, sealing it down; then she stood up. It occurred to her that on her way to post it she could look in at the mini-market next to the Three Blind Mice, and find a present for Kathy, whose birthday fell in a few days' time. She wrapped her shawl around her and opened the bedroom door.

Aunt Nancy stood waiting at the foot of the stairs with an expression of fixed displeasure on her face which could only mean trouble. It was useless trying to evade her. Evidently, she wanted to nag.

"Kate, I'd like a word with you," she said as the young woman slowly descended towards her. "It's about that young man you're knockin' about with."

"Oh, you mean Bruce," said Kate with a mild look, and she fastened the shawl around her neck.

"Now, let's not try to be stupid, Kate," went on her aunt caustically. "You know I can't mean anyone else. You'd better watch yourself, young lady, that's all. I've seen the look in your eyes when you say you're goin' to meet 'im. What you must realise is that this can't go on forever. One of you is goin' to 'ave to put a stop to it. I don't want 'is wife showin' up here and complainin.'"

"I can't see her doing that," retorted Kate, with a glint of amusement. "Unless she doesn't mind being done over, that is."

"You can't be too careful in this life, Kate," warned Aunt Nancy. "So don't go breakin' up other peoples' 'omes."

"But Aunt Nancy, it's not a full relationship, if that's . . ." She began, but the old woman had already taken herself off into the back parts of the house.

Relieved that the argument had gone no further, Kate left her aunt's house and set off down the road, the money for Kathy's present growing warm in her hand."

"Now let's see," she thought to herself, as she entered the shop, to be faced with various boxes of chocolates enticingly wrapped. "No," she decided, turning away from them, "Kathy wouldn't want those as she's trying to slim."

She moved along to a display of initialled pendants which dangled gaudily on a level with her darting eyes. Here she paused longer and hesitated before rejecting the idea on the grounds that she had never seen Kathy wearing jewellery.

But that next counter brought her to something which seemed ideal: a box of fragrant floral stationery. Yes, she thought happily, making her choice at once, Kathy would be pleased with this. She was rightly proud of her capacity to read and write, in which her neighbours and companions were generally so deficient. This would gently flatter that pride and be of real use. So she bought a biro and card to match, exhausting most of her money in the process.

Emerging from the shop, she was, however, somewhat appalled to hear Kathy calling her name. The present she intended for her was clutched under her arm, with only a flimsy paper bag to conceal it from her eyes. Nevertheless, she turned cheerfully as Kathy came running up.

"Talk about entertainment yesterday mornin'," said the younger woman. "You were bleedin' fantastic, Kate. You brought the 'ouse down with your playin', you did."

Kate nodded, smiling. Then she noticed that her young friend's eyes were red, belying the buoyancy of her manner, and she felt concerned at once.

"Have you been crying, Kathy?" she asked.

"Shall we take a walk on the shore?" replied Kathy abruptly. "Or do we just stand 'ere on the street like a pair of lemons?"

Kate nodded again and let the girl go first, slipping through the stunted pillars of the cul-de-sac on the way down to the beach. When they were strolling along, side by side, Kathy spoke again.

"I told you I get low sometimes. I've been to see a doctor about it. 'E says I'm not to worry; when I cry like that, 'e says, it's because I'm suffering from anxiety / depression. 'E's given me some tablets to take."

"At your age, Kathy, for goodness' sake?" cried Kate. "You're so young."

"Oh, it's all right," said Kathy, with a wave of her hand. "It's only a mild form."

"Is he sending you to a specialist about it?"

"Nah!, I'd 'ave to go troopin' all the way to the Medico in the Southern Hemisphere for that, wouldn't I? That's out for a start; it would cost me an arm an' a leg. Anyway, 'e says it's nothin' serious, so it ain't worth worrying about. Once I'm out at work an' am settled it'll all disappear—you'll see. What's that you've got there?" she continued, in childlike curiosity, as she suddenly caught sight of the packet under Kate's arm.

"You told me it was your birthday in the middle of this month," Kate said. "When is it exactly?"

"The 14th," replied Kathy tersely. "That's the day after tomorrow. What about it?"

"Are you celebrating it at all?"

"No way! I'm saving all that for my eighteenth birthday, when I'll get the key to the door an' become an adult in me own right. *That's* when I'll celebrate. Besides," she grimaced, "I'll be at college all day on me birthday; I wouldn't want to miss out on me trainin'. Me mum wouldn't want me to, either."

"Wouldn't she?" asked Kate. "Is your mother that keen for you to start work in the Northern Hemisphere, then?"

"Keen ain't the word for it, mate," remarked Kathy emphatically. "Pushing me all the time, she is. But that's all right, because *I'm* keen too, an' just because it didn't work out for 'er, I don't see why it shouldn't for *me*."

Kate hurriedly withdrew the package from under her arm to change the subject. "I haven't wrapped it yet," she said. "It's your birthday present. You might as well have it now, seeing that it's so close to the day. The card you can have later on. I'll write something on it and post it on to you."

"For me?" exclaimed Kathy, grabbing the bag which Kate now held out to her, and impetuously ripping away at the paper. "Oh, stationery, how lovely!" she gasped, giving Kate a warm hug. "It's because I told you I could write, isn't it?"

"That's right. Well, I'm glad you like them."

The sun came out as she spoke and the grey sea was transformed at once into a dazzling mesh; a crinkled sheet of liquid gold, which faded again as the next cloud loomed. They were drawing near to the end of the beach, Kathy still clutching her present delightedly. Kate asked her if she had ever been through the labyrinth, and the question seemed to astonish her.

"Now, why should I want to do that?" she asked.

"We're only twelve minutes away from the Northern Hemisphere here," explained Kate patiently. "I thought you might have been there before."

"Well, I ain't."

"You want to be a white-collar worker, though, don't you?"

"Yes."

"Well, that's the quarter in which you'll be working, so perhaps you may as well see what it looks like beforehand."

"You mean, go there now?" cried Kathy excitedly. "Both of us?"

"Yes, why not? We'll be frowned upon in our Non-Hemisphere attire, no doubt, but there's nothing like experience to enlighten the mind, is there?" This was said with the faintest touch of sarcasm which Kathy, in her naive enthusiasm, failed to notice.

"It will be excitin'!" she exclaimed. "I can hardly wait!"

"You haven't seen what the quarter's like yet, Kathy," Kate warned her as they moved towards the entrance. "See it first, then become excited. "Come on, it's not far from here."

Chapter Eleven

They emerged among the brash architecture of the New City Road, and Kathy, who had been bubbling with excitement as they walked along the tunnel, now became ecstatic.

"Kate, look!" she cried. "That jeweller's shop next to the employment agency! Ain't it fantastic! An' that magnificent life assurance block—amazin'!"

The life assurance building Kathy had just spoken of was all too familiar to Kate. Its attractive, elegant exterior bore little resemblance to what lay within it. It was the Diamond Life Assurance firm, where Kate had miserably served her sentence as an inexperienced white-collar worker, during her six months of hell. It was where she had spent excruciating hours banging aimlessly at the keys of an obsolete word processor, which shrieked at her if she happened to press the wrong button. It was where, wearily dancing attendance, she had scribbled down messages from someone else's pompous mind, and typed their letters, leaving the spelling unchanged.

In truth, this 'amazin' office block was far from compelling inside; it was falling to pieces. Its walls were grey with neglect; its ancient and decrepit switchboard shrilled endlessly, as if in agony from the need of repair; even the doors creaked on their rusty hinges. Every working surface was littered with the detritus of careless representatives: ash trays filled to the brim, unwashed mugs of half-drunk tea and coffee standing where they could be easily knocked off—it would be up to some menial white-collar worker to clear the resulting mess away. The ink stencil machine, which no bright or willing office member would bother to have repaired, was faulty and could only be operated manually. A thousand copies of the company's magazine would be in demand at the end of each 'exhilarating' month, whereupon the newest employee would be made to undertake the exciting drudgery of getting the monster to work. He would do his utmost to grow familiar with a temperamental roller, and with the gunge of clotted ink that would frequently stick several pages together and eventually clog up the machine. Such was the magnificence of the Diamond Life Assurance office block.

As they turned the corner into Politician's Square, Kathy's eyes were everywhere but on the ground before her feet; catching her toe on the edge of a piece of loose paving, she was thrown to the ground. She did not rise immediately and Kate, squatting down concernedly at her side, noticed that she had lost a little more weight. A businessman carrying a leather briefcase, and who was presumably on his way to work, neatly stepped round her and walked past without breaking stride.

Another, escorting a smartly-dressed woman who was probably his wife, was, however, brought to a halt by this encumbrance barring his way. As Kate helped her young friend to her feet, she was startled to hear him say:

"That's right, keel over at any least little thing. Honestly, these people have no self-control; they just let themselves go. I have no sympathy for them whatsoever."

"Well, what can you expect?" struck in his wife as they marched off. "She's a down and out, isn't she? They're all lazy and half asleep down there. At least," she added, pointing to the gutter and enjoying her little joke," she fell over in the appropriate spot."

From Kathy's expression, Kate could see that she was aghast. As for herself, such behaviour only reinforced what she had come to expect.

The smug couple moved on. However, before they had gone from sight, exactly the same accident prostrated the wife a little further up the street. Instantly her husband flew to her aid.

"My poor darling!" he cried. "What an awful thing! Here, let me help you. Are you all right?"

"I'm not sure," she murmered as he knelt by her side. "I feel rather faint." The businessman hugged her in a sickly fashion.

"All right, Sarah, I'll tell you what we'll do. I'll take you to the hospital, just to be on the safe side; I'll go into work late."

"But what about your lunch, Roy? I haven't prepared it for you yet."

"Forget lunch, darling," he told her with breathless sincerity. "I'll come home and cook it for us both. And leave the housework—I'll do it this evening."

"Oh, Roy!" The woman put on a gratingly feminine voice. "You're *so* understanding!"

Suddenly Kate felt Kathy freeing herself from her restraining arm, and she was appalled to hear her shout after the retreating couple: "Two-faced bastards!"

"Kathy!" she whispered in a tone of mild reproof. Her young companion swung round wildly.

"Look, Kate," she said fiercely, "I felt rotten when I collapsed on that pavement—absolutely rotten! There wasn't a mark on that slut when she fell, an' that bleedin' 'usband of 'ers—having told me *I* was making a fuss—actually offered to take 'er to the 'ospital! I bet *she* ain't been raped. She was makin' a right meal of it, and that bastard goes an' slates *me*!"

"I know she was making a fuss, Kathy," answered Kate in a sympathetic tone, "but she was his wife; he felt responsible for her."

"Responsible, my foot!" cried Kathy. "She's a grown woman with arms, an' legs an' a mind, ain't she? Treating her like a doll, after what he said to me—that's what makes me sick!"

"I can see your point, Kathy, "said Kate, "but if she were really an adult, she would never had made such a scene. It's a little game they play, don't you see?"

"In which I'm the football, I suppose?"

Kate stole a glance at her face, as she wondered if her ruse of bringing her naive young friend here to give her a foretaste of Northern Hemisphere ways was actually working.

"Now you see what I mean about the Northern Hemisphere," she said softly. "Perhaps this will change your mind about wanting to work here."

Kathy compressed her lips. "Why should it? What on earth 'as me job got to do with one woman fallin' in the street? I shan't be anywhere near the street when I'm sittin' be'ind a word processor, tappin' away."

"They're all like that, Kathy, don't you understand?" said Kate, trying to press home her advantage, though she felt her opportunity was slipping away."

Kathy looked more vexed than ever. "I don't know what you're on about, Kate. It'll be just an office, a few desks and a word processor. What's the matter with you, anyway? You're sayin' I shouldn't become a typist, aren't you? Are you tryin' to stop me getting anywhere with me life? You've got a nerve! It's the land of opportunity, anyone can see that. Just because you had a bad experience . . ."

"Kathy," interrupted Kate, "I did exactly as you're planning to do; so did my aunt; nearly every literate young Non-Hemisphere girl has the same dream. A white-collar worker's position in the Northern Hemisphere is seen as an escape, a haven; but it's not—it's just another dead end. There was gossip which circulated around the office about me; within six months I was told to leave. Following that I went for interview after interview, when I could hardly get past the door; finally, one interviewer disclosed to me that I'd been blacklisted. My records were so bad, he told me, that I would never be employed in the Northern Hemisphere again."

"But you were just unlucky!" protested Kathy vehemently. "It don't mean it's goin' to 'appen to me. You're just jealous because your career as a white-collar worker never worked out for you! At least me mum's not jealous," she added indignantly. "At least *she* ain't tryin' to put me off."

And Kate stood forlornly in that busy street, knowing that her mission had failed.

Chapter Twelve

Kathy had given her the number if her house, and though she had never been there before, it did not prove hard for Kate to find it. The shabby house fronts all looked alike, but the numbers had been painted up, and though these were now peeling, enough remained to guide her to the place.

It was Kathy's birthday. Kate knew she would not be at home, but it was not actually Kathy whom she wanted to see. The tall, brusque woman who opened the door was far from friendly.

"Yes, I'm 'er mother," she said curtly, in answer to Kate's question. "What's it to you?"

"I'm Kate Brannigan," said Kate, discomforted by this hostile reception. "I expect Kathy has mentioned me to you. I wondered if I could have a word with you."

"You'd better come in then," said Mrs Fellowes, reluctantly inching the door open. "Go through to the kitchen. I've been tidying up. You can sit down if you like."

Kate preceded the surly woman down a tunnel of drabness and squalor. In the greasy room at the far end, she obediently took a seat by the old table, while Kathy's mother, her hands placed firmly on her hips, remained standing.

"What's this about then? I haven't got all day."

Kate sighed, dreading the ordeal, but knowing that she had to go through with it for Kathy's sake.

"It's about Kathy, Mrs Fellowes. I'm very concerned about her."

"Oh yes? There's nothin' about Kathy that's botherin' *me* at the moment," replied the obstreperous woman.

"I don't think she's really happy about the shorthand / typist's course she's taking. If you must know, I feel it's making her ill without her realising it."

"Oh yes?"

"Mrs. Fellowes." Kate massaged the back of her neck. "What I really mean, Mrs. Fellowes, is that I think it would be best if Kathy abandoned the thought of going out to work as a white-collar worker in the Northern Hemisphere."

"Do you now? What gives you the gall to say a thing like that?"

"She's not well, Mrs Fellowes. Are you aware that she is suffering from a mild form of anxiety / depression?"

"Yes, I know that."

"Then aren't you worried? I mean, this is your daughter we're talking about; not just anybody."

"Who are you to tell me 'ow to manage me own daughter?" retorted Mrs Fellowes. "Kathy 'as the chance of a good career; something a lot of young Non-Hemisphere folk don't 'ave. I want 'er to prove 'erself, and so does she. She's perfectly 'appy to become a shorthand / typist; and so am I."

"Yes," said Kate, becoming a little impatient, "but what about her mental state?"

"Er mental state!" cried Mrs Fellowes indignantly. "Kathy ain't mental! She's just been feelin' a bit low lately, that's all."

"I understand," said Kate, in as sweet a tone as she could manage "that you yourself worked in a Northern Hemisphere office as a shorthand / typist some years ago?"

"Yes, I did. What of it?"

"Didn't that experience make you aware of how the Northern Hemisphere treats and regards Non-Hemisphere white-collar workers? Surely you must have noticed the tension that exists between the classes?"

"There's tensions all over," retorted Mrs Fellowes. "It's a part of life, ain't it?"

"Kathy tells me that you weren't kept on; yet I'm sure it can't have been through any lack of personal qualities."

"Kathy's going to make her own way and prove herself," said the woman resolutely. "Goin' out there an' showin' she can hold down a job will actually cure her of 'er depression. I really believe that. There's too much negative talk. What happened to me or you or whoever, makes no difference."

"I didn't come here to argue with you, Mrs Fellowes," said Kate, doing her best to remain calm, "but this has to be said. I am warning you not to send Kathy to a Northern Hemisphere office. She has emotional difficulties. She lost her father when she was only a child. Worse, she tells me that she was raped as a teenager. I shudder to think how she will cope in the Northern Hemisphere. I can tell you now that, far from helping her, she'll be thrown back on the scrap heap in a short time; the experience could have a devastating effect."

"Get along with you!" cackled Mrs Fellowes. "I suppose you're setting yourself up as the example for her to follow—drawing your dole money and hanging about the streets? I reckon you need your brains testing, young lady; you ought to come down and live in the real world like the rest of us."

"You can keep your 'real world'," replied Kate quietly. "I'm quite content to sit in my ivory tower. But if I see a person going wrong, or making the same mistakes I made, I rush out and try to stop them. I am telling you that Kathy is going to be badly hurt."

"Yah!" snorted Mrs. Fellowes, waving a derisive arm. "Cloud Cukoo Land, you said it yourself. Condemned yourself out of your own mouth, you did. You and your airs and graces! All very well in the Eastern 'Emisphere, I've no doubt, but they're no bleedin' good 'ere. Now, I've 'eard all I want to 'ear from the likes of you, so kindly take yourself off."

"As you wish." Kate dragged herself to her feet. At the entrance to the passage, she turned again only to be confronted by the woman's pointing hand.

"You know where the front door is," said Mrs Fellowes jeerily. "I 'ope you know 'ow to walk through an ordinary door. I know you're only used to ivory towers!"

Kate regained the street, blazing with indignation. She slammed the gate to give some vent to her feelings, and marched off. But soon she slowed to a more rueful pace. She knew the influence that Mrs Fellowes had over her daughter, and the affection that Kathy professed to have for the unamiable woman. Now, by her failure, she wondered if this would mark the end of the friendship between Kathy are herself.

Chapter Thirteen

"I believe it will be your birthday soon," said Bruce, as he sat with Kate on the sofa in her aunt's front room, his mac lying casually folded over the shabby armrest beside him. Somewhere in the background, Aunt Nancy was clattering as she went about her household chores.

"Yes! How did you know that?"

"I think you told me yourself." He moved to put his arm around her, but she instinctively retreated.

"We have only just met," she said warily.

"That makes no difference," he averred. "It's the intimacy of the relationship that counts."

Kate immediately felt that he was putting pressure on her; she changed the subject. "You were saying . . . about my birthday?"

"Oh yes." He took his arm away. "I was going to ask you what kind of food you like."

"Ground pork; ground beef, with fruit and vegetables," answered Kate, sighing at the memories. "You know: the usual Eastern Hemisphere food."

"I imagine you don't get the opportunity to eat much of that nowadays," commented Bruce; at which point the rattling and banging from the kitchen suddenly seemed to increase.

"No, that's true. The Non-Hemisphere diet is rather limited: things like vegetable pie and marrow soup. Otherwise it's just something on toast."

"I wondered why you didn't have much colour in your cheeks," he said, stroking her left cheekbone with the tips of his fingers.

And once again, Kate was torn emotionally by even this light contact, and she was actually relieved when her aunt popped her head round the door, putting an end to such intimacies. She came bearing lunch, in the shape of a plate of lentil loaf and a tureen of steaming vegetable broth.

Kate served, and they all chewed meditatively for a while before Bruce broke the awkward silence.

"As I was saying, Kate, does Northern Hemisphere food appeal to you at all?"

"Well, I'm not much acquainted with it," she admitted, keeping her eyes lowered. "But I loved the beef in red wine that we had at the restaurant in Politician's Square last month."

"Then may I ask you to join me there again on your birthday?"

"All right." Kate smiled. "Yes, that would be lovely. Thank you."

"Does your wife know about this?" said Aunt Nancy, scowling fiercely in Bruce's direction.

"Aunt Nancy, please!"

"Well," stated her aunt bluntly, "'e knows 'ow I feel about the situation. You're too rash for your own good, Kate Brannigan."

"Not long now before Kate goes to visit her mother in the Eastern Hemisphere, Miss Brannigan," said Bruce to Aunt Nancy, rapidly changing the subject.

"Yes, and a waste of time that is, if you ask me," she responded sourly. "It only means me niece 'as a taste of the comforts she can no longer enjoy."

"That's true, Aunt Nancy," said Kate, painfully aware that it was, "but don't forget, the main point of my going is to pay my respects to my mother. It would be unfair to expect her to come here. It would not be safe, anyway."

Aunt Nancy grunted derisively. "I expect it weren't safe for you when you first come over to the Non-'Emisphere, either," she said drily. She seemed to be in one of her immovable, cantankerous moods.

Bruce tried again. "How's Kathy, by the way? Are you seeing her these days?"

"Not so much," confessed Kate. "Hardly at all this month, except in the Three Blind Mice on Saturdays, and even then she avoids me."

"Have you two fallen out then?"

"No, I wouldn't say that. But her mother's taken against me, and presumably Kathy has too."

"Serves you right, Kate Brannigan," struck in Aunt Nancy, "for pokin' your nose into other people's affairs. If Kathy wants to make a mess of 'er life, then that's up to 'er."

There was a grain of truth in this, too, thought Kate, biting her lip and not responding.

Bruce glanced at his watch, and gave an exclamation. "Miss Brannigan, you'll have to excuse me. That was most enjoyable, but now I must return to my duties."

"That's all right, young man," said Aunt Nancy. "But if you'll take my advice, you'd do better for all concerned if you returned to your wife instead, once in a while. You know how I feel on the subject; and so does me niece."

"I'll bear that in mind, Miss Brannigan," he told her, rising swiftly and collecting his mac.

"I'll walk you to the labyrinth, Bruce," said Kate.

"Spooning like young lovers," shot Aunt Nancy after them as they made their way through the passage to the front door.

They followed the path from the cul-de-sac down to the beach.

"I take it that your aunt disapproves of our relationship because I'm a married man," said Bruce.

"That's right," replied Kate in a vexed tone. "And she's always telling me to mind *my* own business!"

"Perhaps it runs in the family," said Bruce slyly.

"Oh, Bruce—how dare you!" And they both burst out laughing. At the entrance to the tunnel, he gripped her hand warmly.

"I'll see you on the evening of your birthday, then, Kate," he said. "God bless until then."

"Not too long, is it?" she replied; but he assured her that any absence from her was too long for him, and that pleased her.

They parted, and Kate was about to return to Terminal Lane, when she saw a familiar figure come hurrying out of the labyrinth. It was Kathy. She was not sure whether to approach her or not, but, feeling how awkward it would be for them both to follow the same road without speaking, she tentatively called her name. To her relief, Kathy did not seem unfriendly.

"Oh, Kate! I've just been for a job interview in the Northern 'Emisphere. I'm wearin' me mac."

"So, I see. It's a bit early for an interview, isn't it?" asked Kate. "I thought you still had a month of your course to do?"

"I 'ave," said Kathy perkily, "but the firm told me they could wait until the middle of next month to take me on, as the girl I'll be replacin' 'as given a month's notice."

She smiled exultantly; there was a heaviness under her eyes which Kate did not fail to detect.

"You look tired, Kathy", she said anxiously. "Have you been under any sort of strain since I last saw you?"

"If you mean the anxiety / depression thing," came the cheerful reply, "I've been feelin' so great lately that I've been off me tablets for an 'ole three weeks now. Brilliant, ain't it?"

Kate did not reply.

Kathy began again. "Sorry I ain't been to see you since . . ." She hesitated. "The fact is," she said confidentially, "me mum didn't like you comin' to 'er 'ouse an' dictatin' to 'er about what I should be doin', see; so she told me to cool off a bit."

"Your mother does appear to dominate you rather," said Kate warily. "I got that impression. It's *your* life, Kathy—no one else's."

"I know it's my life," Kathy replied, "an' I *am* leading it in me own way; an' I'll be even more able to do what I want if I earn me own money, won't I? That's what me mum says, anyway. You and me, Kate," she went on brightly, "we'll be able to knock around together all I like once I get a place of me own. They pay well, those Northern 'Emisphere firms."

Kate stared helplessly away. The lighthouse stood illuminated in this light.

"You'll be goin' to see your mum in the Eastern 'Emisphere soon, "said Kathy. "I expect I'll have found meself a job by the time you get back."

"So I won't be seeing you until after that?" questioned Kate.

"No, best not. Wait till I make sure I've got a job. And I'll give you your birthday present later, too, when you come back from your mother's, if you don't mind."

Kate was puzzled, but she gave a faint nod.

"Anyway, better be off now," said Kathy hurriedly. "Got me exams next week; I need to put in some swottin'. 'Ave a nice Christmas, won't you, Kate?"

"Yes, and you too, Kathy!" called Kate as the girl strode on ahead, leaving her dallying and anxious on the shore.

Chapter Fourteen

The brief sunlight of Christmas Eve gleamed on the sleek, metallic body of the Electro-Train, as it sped into the Eastern Hemisphere terminus. Kate stepped down, breathing the air of that quarter which once she had been at liberty to roam. Passing the barrier with the other passengers, she entered the transparent lift which shot her straight down to street level. To her foreigner's eyes the forum looked vast and magical, wreathed with Christmas lights and surrounded with glistening snow.

She made haste to enter this fairyland, where tall spruces stood adorned with tinsel, and where a snow-decked toy stall was doing a brisk trade.

Close by the largest tree of all stood a young girl dressed in white. She was no more than a child, but she was beautiful, with the face of a fairy princess; and in her hand she held a wand with a bright silver star glowing at its tip. If Kate had been told she had stepped straight off the tree, she would have accepted that. Something about the child seemed to beckon her to draw near; and forward she went, so enchanted that she forgot to be reserved.

"You look beautiful," she told her, almost breathlessly. "Thank you." The girl was modest and sweet. "You're beautiful, too."

"Your father," said Kate, the tears welling up in her eyes. "I bet he's proud of you and that he'll buy you a lovely present for Christmas. You'll appreciate his love for you, won't you?"

It was doubtful if the child understood this. She was too young; she had yet to be tainted with loss. Perhaps, reflected Kate, love has to be withdrawn or destroyed before one can realise what it is. Still she pressed on.

"I bet you had Christmas decorations up at school. Do you like school? Are they giving you a good education? Is that where you've just come from? Have you been in the nativity play? That's such a beautiful dress. Are you a fairy or an angel?"

The child stared at her with eyes that seemed to search her very soul. She did not speak, and it was impossible to tell how she regarded this stranger who had come so impetuously to talk to her. But she was not frightened or hostile, and Kate, driven by some desperate need, went on trying to communicate with her.

"I expect you and your family will spend Christmas in your Eastern Hemisphere villa, will you? It'll be Christmas Day tomorrow. Are you looking forward to it? I'm sure you love your family very much. Tell me what it's like to have a father—a guardian who can guide and comfort you and put you on the right path. Tell me, please!"

But the child did not reply and Kate, hearing a sound behind her, turned to look into the eyes of a young, aesthetic-looking couple, their arms full of toys, who were bearing down on her. The child was inscrutable, but her parents' eyes were full of doubt and anger and loathing. Suddenly the mother stopped and drew the child to her, while the father stood menacingly close.

"We can't leave you along for five minutes!" chided the mother. "How many times have I told you not to speak to strangers? I thought the first thing they taught you at school was of the dangers of class tension in the society of today?"

"She's nothing to do with us!" put in the father, looking daggers at Kate, who had not moved. "Come on, let's go! Do as I say! You should be ashamed!" This last comment was directed at Kate.

"Please," implored Kate, taking the child's hand, "I mean you no harm. Tell me how you feel inside with a family to guide you!"

But it was too late. If the child understood, she was not saying; her parents hovered like frightened birds of prey around the disturbed next of their young one. The father reached out a talon-like hand

and broke Kate's grip, his sharp nails driving into her knuckles, while the child, almost absorbed in the mother's embrace, was hurried off. Soon they were three blurs receding towards the forum entrance, and Kate was left alone, sobbing and nursing her hand in that vast space.

But it was not the physical pain which had precipitated her tears. It was the shock of rejection, the inevitability of her exclusion from the family circle. That refined-looking couple could have been her own parents, before she had been forced into exile from this place; the lovingly shielded child could have been herself.

Her actual homecoming, after this, was bound to be a disappointment. Her mother's villa stood not far away, within a patterned courtyard, in a row of others of a like kind. She was late and the door was almost instantly opened as she pressed the bell. But the tall, middle-aged woman with the kindly round face who greeted her, was someone Kate had never met before.

"Well, well! Don't tell me: you must be Kate," she said, with a warm smile. "You're just as your mother described you, except that you are far prettier than I ever could have imagined you would be. Come in out of the cold," she added, leading her inside. "Your mother will be with us in a minute. I'll just go and tell her you're here. I'm Deborah, her new neighbour, by the way. We have arranged to spend the whole of Christmas in each other's company. I'm a widow like she is, but I have no family. But enough about me; I'll go and tell your mother."

And off she went, leaving Kate alone in the guestroom. She looked about her with melancholic eyes. The spacious garden beyond the veranda had a stark look. It was the low season; but even in high summer she doubted if it ever recovered to the abundance she had known as a child. Weeds, great dried webs of them, had invaded the beds and overhung them like some monstrous spider's work; the neat walks were soiled and neglected. In the centre, the fountain still flowed, but timorously, weeping over the side of its slimy bowl.

The smell of roasted game came wafting from the kitchen; her mother, arm in arm with Deborah, approached.

"You're late," she said, releasing herself from Deborah in order to give Kate a brief, welcoming hug. "You'd better remove your mac. Here's your stola, which you can wear throughout your stay." She produced the bright yellow garment from under her arm; Kate nearly cried when she saw it. It had been a present from her parents on her fifteenth birthday. It had been freshly pressed, and it suddenly occurred to Kate that it would never get much use.

"We'll have lunch at once, if you're ready," went on Mrs Tiberius. "I have prepared roast partridge, which I hope is to your liking. It's so long since you have lived with me that I have forgotten what your tastes in food are."

"I'll go and serve it up," offered Deborah, smiling kindly. "I'm sure that you and your mother have a lot to talk about."

"No!" called Kate's mother, holding out a hand to stop her. "There's no need to put yourself to any trouble, Deborah. You are a guest in this villa, too, you know."

"Don't be silly, Miriam," chided her friend. "I'd be only too pleased to assist you with *something*." And off she glided, leaving mother and daughter alone.

Kate saw with a shock that her mother's hair had turned completely grey since she had last seen her. She looked frail and worn, and prematurely aged. She reflected that the emotional strain of having lost her husband and daughter within a matter of months had insidiously taken its toll. She started to unbutton her mac, revealing her shabby Non-Hemisphere attire beneath.

Mrs Tiberius said calmly: "Once you're changed into your stola, we must make our way into the dining room."

"I'll go and change then," said Kate, frozen a little by her mother's reticence.

"Wait!" Mrs Tiberius called her back. "There's something I want to tell you." Kate turned expectantly. "Deborah has suggested that the three of us pay a visit to the theatre in town early this evening—then we'll go on the attend Christmas Eve mass at the temple."

"That sounds nice," said Kate, biting her lip. "Yes, I'd like that. What are we going to see?"

"'Dr Faustus', by Christopher Marlowe," replied her mother, some colour flowing into her gaunt cheeks. "It's about a doctor of medicine who sells his soul to the Devil in exchange for wealth and supernatural powers."

"Yes, I know", said Kate resignedly. "I studied the play in my last year at school, but didn't get the chance to sit the exam."

Chapter Fifteen

Kathy ran into her in Terminal Lane on the second Saturday after her return, as Kate was on her way to perform as usual at the Three Blind Mice.

"Oi, Kate!" said the girl in her inimitable accent, but seeming, Kate thought, genuinely pleased at this meeting. "It ain't arf nice to see you again! 'Ow are you? Did you enjoy your trip to the Eastern 'Emisphere Christmas time?"

"Yes," said Kate. "It was a change of scenery, at least."

"'Ow's Bruce?" the other girl continued conversationally, as they walked along together.

"Bruce is fine," replied Kate. "He says he missed me over Christmas.

"I'm really late today," chuckled Kathy, nonchalantly. "I should 'ave got here a couple of hours ago."

"I didn't see you last week," said Kate. "At least you may have been there, but I didn't notice you."

"No, I weren't there!" Kathy's eyes sparkled with amusement. "An' if the landlord creates, then it's just tough for 'im, ain't it, 'cause from next week, I'll 'ave jacked the job in, anyway."

"Why's that, Kathy?"

"'Cause I got that job at the insurance firm," announced Kathy, smiling with elation. "You remember: the one I'd just been to for an interview when I met you by the labyrinth before you went to see your mother? I knew I was in with a chance. Well, I start next week. The people there ain't arf classy, Kate. It's like a different world. I'll be able to afford lots of new clothes an' everythin'. Beats bein' stuck in the 'ouse or wanderin' the streets all day."

"You're looking much better, Kathy," Kate told her. "You were so thin the last time I saw you. Have you finally found a man or something?"

"No, but somethin' tells me it won't be long before I do." Kathy grinned. "Things are goin' to change from now on. From next week, it's goin' to be nobody else's life I'll be livin' but me own; so I'll be earnin' an' payin' me own way; so me mum will 'ave to give me more say, won't she?"

They had reached the entrance to the inn. "How did your mother react when you told her you'd got the job?" Kate asked.

"Oh, thrilled to bits, she was," replied Kathy, holding open the swing door for Kate to pass through with her bulky guitar. "I reckon she's proud of me at last."

"How about your exams, Kathy?"

"Great!" the girl exclaimed proudly. "I got through them all except for Secretarial Procedures—that's tact an' all that—but I should be able to pick that up on the job. I also got a certificate in word processin', though the insurance firm 'as different word processors from the one the college 'ad. Still, the firm told me they would cross-train me—so there should be no problems on that count. Oh, Kate!" she cried, raising her voice as they pushed through the noisy, crowded inn. "I can't believe this is 'appenin to me. I'm so thrilled that even me depression's disappeared—vanished into thin air!"

Mr Allinson, the landlord, had seen them and was coming over, but he had eyes only for Kathy, and Kate began to feel concerned for her young friend again; then she saw that he was looking far from pleased.

"Well, if it ain't Miss Fellowes!" he remarked in mock surprise. "It's so nice to 'ave the pleasure of your company once again. And where did you get to last Saturday?"

"I'm preparin' meself for bigger and better things, if you must know, Mr Allinson," retorted Kathy, without a trace of guilt or shame.

"Ho, ho, ho!" said the landlord coldly. He turned straight to Kate, who had been staggered by Kathy's response. "What's your friend been up to, love?"

Kate stammered and began to say lamely that she was not sure, when Kathy struck in boldly. "I've found a full-time job."

"A full-time job," he echoed, staring at her. "In this quarter?"

"Of course it ain't in this quarter," replied Kathy sharply. "It's in the Northern 'Emisphere. I'm goin' to be a white-collar worker."

She had spoken carelessly and out load; instantly the whole inn fell silent. A table full of gossiping spinsters all turned their heads her way.

"Not so loud, Kathy!" Kate pleaded with her. "Don't let everyone in here know!"

But it was too late for that. One of the women, heavily-built and not the kind one would choose to cross, rose to her feet.

"You mean to say you're goin' to work amongst all them vile bitches?" she railed at Kathy.

"An' why not?" snapped the girl. "What's wrong with tryin' to better meself? I'm not asking you to come with me, am I?"

"Don't worry, dearie," sneered the woman. "I wouldn't work in the Northern 'Emisphere for all the tea in China. I wouldn't be seen dead in that rotten, biased quarter. And it's dead you'll be, my fine young woman, and nailed down in your coffin before you better yourself there!"

"Now then, ladies," said Mr Allinson, looking anxious, "that'll be quite enough for one mornin'. Any more of that and I'll have to ask you to sort it out outside. You've been warned, Kathy!" He made a gesture to indicate that she should move to her place behind the bar. Meanwhile, the other woman had seated herself once more among her cronies.

But Kathy did not move. Kate, obscurely aware of the explosion that was about to follow, nervously started to unzip her guitar case. Kathy had her hands on her hips; her head was defiantly thrown back.

"Were you orderin' me out of this inn a moment ago?" she asked the landlord aggressively.

Mr Allinson pursed his lips. "Look, love," he said half-apologetically, "you have to realise that no employee is indispensable. If you want to pick a fight, it don't exactly create a harmonious atmosphere—especially in a place like this, now does it?"

"Well," retorted Kathy, stamping furiously, "I don't need you or anyone else in this inn any more than you need me. You can go and get yourself another barmaid right now—because from next week, I won't be needin' *your* paltry wages!" And with that she marched towards the exit doors, and punched them open with her fists. "An' I've no time for jealous old cows, either!" she shouted, throwing the spinsters a malignant glance before flouncing out of the inn.

The doors crashed to and there was a moment of silence; everyone seemed too surprised to speak. Everyone that is, except the aggrieved older woman, whose mutterings grew more vocal like a rapidly approaching storm.

Mr Allinson stepped into the breach with wagging finger raised; he looked as if he feared he would have a riot on his hands.

"Now that's enough! Quieten down! This is a respectable pub, and I aim to keep it that way. I don't want no trouble, right? Now," he went on, "here's a lovely young lady, Kate Brannigan, who's waitin' to entertain us with her songs. She's been very patient. Are we goin' to hear her or not?"

"Yes!" cried various voices of the regulars.

"Then let's settle down and enjoy ourselves." He produced a large handkerchief and wiped his forehead. As he passed Kate on his way to the back room, he said in a lower voice: "Over to you, love."

Several people clapped in anticipation as Kate leant forward, gripping the cylindrical microphone.

"It's so nice to be appreciated by such a warm and friendly crowd," she said, her voice wavering a little. "I've a song here that you won't have heard before, which I hope you'll like. I wrote it myself. It's called 'Timeless.'"

Order was now fully restored, and the attention of the audience was centred on the singer as she strummed her guitar. But the singer's thoughts, though she gave a flawless performance, were not on the words or the chords. She kept seeing Kathy in her mind. And the girl seemed like a comet to her: beautiful in its fury, rushing to its ruin.

Chapter Sixteen

"More bleedin' bills," moaned Aunt Nancy as she bent down to collect the afternoon post. "I 'ardly use the electricity, yet the bills keep going up. Oh well, it never rains but it pours, as the saying goes. Ah, an' 'ere's a letter for *you*, Kate, so you may as well take it now," she added, handing her niece a little white envelope, the edges of which were covered with a bright mosaic pattern. Kate could tell by the postmark—a pillared temple almost obscuring the stamp—and by the rounded italic writing that it was from Rebecca. She tore it open in agitation.

"It's a wedding invitation," she said flatly to Aunt Nancy, who was hovering inquisitively nearby. "From Rebecca."

"Don't sound too pleased about it, will you?" was the sarcastic comment in reply. "By the way, what time are you expectin' Kathy over?"

"Five fifteen. She's coming straight round from work." The letter from Rebecca was folded round the card, but Aunt Nancy still hovered infuriatingly.

"'Ow's she gettin' on in the job, anyway?"

"Oh, she's only been there a month," said Kate, "and I've not seen much of her; but as far as I know, she seems to be getting on all right, apart from one or two problems concerning the word processor."

"A month's nothin' to go by," remarked Aunt Nancy sourly. "Let's 'ope she's still as 'appy in a few months' time." And then, thankfully, she thudded upstairs and Kate was able to pursue Rebecca's letter undisturbed.

> *"Dear Kate,"* it began. *"I sincerely hope you had a superb Christmas and that your mother and Deborah enjoyed it just as much. I spent mine at my parent's villa in Lancaster, my last Christmas as a free, single young woman! The villa which Judah and I purchased at the end of last year is now decorated and almost completely furnished. I'll have my parents to stay with US next Christmas.*

> *"This letter is to confirm the date and venue of my wedding: Wednesday 2nd May at twelve o'clock at the 'Rubicon' Temple, Lancaster. I do hope that you and your mother will be able to attend. I know Judah would be happy to meet you. I have also*

taken the opportunity to invite Deborah, as she is such a good and loyal friend to your mother—a great comfort to her when otherwise her life might at times seem rather lonely.

"What super news about Bruce! It appears that you are finally beginning to see the light after that traumatic attack ten years ago. Let's hope that wedding bells will be heard peeling forth in your direction in the not too distant future.

"Please write soon to inform me if you are able to come to the wedding. I do hope so. I send my fondest wishes to Aunt Nancy, Kathy and Bruce—and to yourself, of course.

"Write soon . . . . Rebecca."

Kate folded the letter, placing it back inside the envelope which she left temporarily propped up against the drawing room mantelpiece. Furtively, the clock on the wall slid its hand a fraction to the right. Aunt Nancy came tramping downstairs, wrapped up warmly against the elements."

"I'll be off now, Kate," she said. "Seein' a friend for the evenin'. I should be back around nine. Give Kathy my regards, won't you?"

The front door slammed behind her and Kate, left alone, made for the drawing room armed with a duster, which, moodily, she attacked the more obvious surfaces. Thinking of Kathy, she called to mind her own experiment with Red Liquor at her first meeting with Bruce; and how vile it had tasted. It was not Red Liquor—it was blood; a fitting emblem for that Hemisphere. Bruce had said it was an acquired taste—and how right he was.

Kathy would be buoyant at this time, she thought, if her career conformed to the usual pattern. She would be awash with cash, in contrast to her more straitened days in the Non-Hemisphere. The remorseless process of rejection would not yet have started in her case. That cruelty still lay a few months ahead for her.

They were all leeches and vampires over there! They drew their sustenance from strong young bodies and from hopes not yet broken by the corruption of the world. They needed an endless supply of victims who, when they had finished with them, they spat out. They spread ruin; they did not care. Kate herself had had to harden her heart after their treatment of her. Even now the ground had a habit of vanishing from under her feet, leaving her, at moments of crisis, feeling helpless and exposed. How much worse it would be for Kathy when the time came; for she, for all her appearance of toughness, was a very sensitive plant.

The dusting bored Kate and when the constant bending had made her back ache, she threw down the cloth and climbed the stairs to her room. There she stood for a long time studying her reflection in the large mirror inset in the door of her wardrobe. Turning sideways, she ran her fingers down the knobbly bones of her spine, frowning as her glance rested on the slight hunch of her shoulders. To an outsider she would have seemed a picture of beauty with her flowing hair, her soft eyes and her smooth and pearly complexion—but she would acknowledge none of these things. It was as if she were afraid to do so, as if she felt menaced even by this pleasing presence which seemed detached to her from the anguish of her soul.

The sea was in the back of her picture. It flowed over her reflection, swathing her, wrapping her in its spectral veil. The tide was the master of her moods; lying on the moist, warm sand, she was like a shell that a stronger wave had cast up. She had been held in Ocean's embrace; his horizon-wide scent all about her; in his deepest caverns was her home . . ."

It was difficult to live in a world of prejudice and harsh isolation, where Hemisphere clashed with Hemisphere. But in one vivid moment, she saw those barriers go down. The labyrinths crumbled, swallowed greedily by the encroaching sea. House walls, strong and weak, succumbed to the conqueror as he rode the waves of his own creation, fierce and unchecked! Glamour and squalor, fine clothes and foul liquors, were all swept along. He invaded the disintegrating offices, plucking out computers and files and depositing them on factory floors. Guitars twanged in churches, crucifixes flashed in neon over ritzy nightclubs. No one was single or frightened; all functions, all classes merged.

She felt a liquid mass around her ankles, and found herself at the fringes of the sea; the languid air of late afternoon drew her further and further into the depths. Without pain, the one noble element wrapped itself around her. Dreamily she felt it swirl, rising, around her waist, and smelt in her nostrils the tang of the waves. She felt she could walk straight on into Paradise . . .

The sudden sharp voice startled her and made her eyes fly open.

"Kate! What on earth are you doin'? The tide's comin' in! What are you tryin' to do—drown yourself?"

It was Kathy; recognisable by her voice, though not by her form, which was hazy in this purple light. Kate shrugged and walked out of the sea.

"What brings you out here, Kathy?" she asked politely, joining her on the shore.

"I could ask you the same question." Kathy sounded irritated. "I went to 'ave a chat with the lighthouse keeper if you must know. I often do nowadays; I was on my way up to your place."

"Yes, I was waiting for you. I've made some supper. My aunt's out for the evening, so we can have a good long talk. Are you all right, Kathy? You sound a bit on edge." It was impossible to make out her friend's face in this twilight. They both turned and walked along the beach.

"I'm not hungry," grunted Kathy. "I shan't want anything. I can't eat; it makes me feel sick."

"For Heaven's sake, Kathy, what do you mean?"

"I don't want any supper, right?" snapped the younger woman. "Yes, we'll talk, but don't try to force any food on me."

Kate was surprised, but she made no reply, and they continued on their way towards the house in silence.

Chapter Seventeen

"It ain't bleedin' fair!" Kathy suddenly blurted out. "I feel betrayed, I do."

They were sitting in Aunt Nancy's front room, Kate having changed out of her wet things. Her first look at Kathy's face in the light had been a shock: she appeared drained, washed out, suddenly much older. Kate's heart bled for her.

"Betrayed about what, Kathy?" she asked her.

"About forkin' out for a college course and strugglin' to pass an exam in word processin', only to find I 'ave to be trained all over again because the firm operates a different system, that's what," said the girl petulantly. "I went out to work to leave me days of studyin' be'ind me; not to go on WP courses for the rest of me life."

"You must be patient, Kathy," said Kate, cringing inwardly as she spoke. "You've only been at the firm for a month. It's early days yet."

Kathy ignored her and ploughed on in the same irritated spirit.

"There's this switchboard girl in our office—born in the Northern 'Emisphere, of course. She's 'ardly ever in; she's always late. When she *does* turn up, she spends 'arf an hour in the 'Ladies' dolling 'erself up before she actually gets be'ind the switchboard—an' I'm expected to take all the calls for 'er. I ain't been trained for that. I keep cuttin' everybody off because she won't show me 'ow to work it. Will she stir her fat behind to give me a hand? Will she 'ell! Yet the manager—a man—never ticks her off for bein' late; though 'e soon pulls *me* up for any little thing I done wrong. What's the matter with me?" she asked ruefully. "Do men find me ugly, or somethin'?"

It was not a question requiring an answer, and Kate, though she felt her pain, did not reply.

"That switchboard girl 'as lung trouble," she continued, "'an' she smokes like a chimney an' makes 'erself worse, then spends days off work. Sometimes she ain't even ill; she just skives off. When she gets back after a week, she's smokin' as usual, and sure enough, she starts coughin' again. Instead of the manager takin' a firm 'and, 'e only goes an' tells 'er she should still be in bed. I ask you! Not that she's probably been in bed, unless it's with a man. An' there am I, 'avin' to spend nearly all the days leave I get, seein' the doctor for me anxiety / depression! But that, of course," she ended bitterly, "is all me own fault!"

"You're telling *me* all this, Kathy," said Kate. "But have you discussed it with anyone in the office?"

"No, but I'm bleedin' well goin' to," said the other hotly. "I always do my bit and I don't mind hard work; but when it comes to prejudice and injustice, I bleedin' blow me top. I don't care who knows—why should I? I ain't got nothin' to hide. If I'm spat on, I'll spit back. Men 'ave been nothin' but bastards to me in the past, so what do I owe them, anyway? Why the 'ell should I go crawlin' around *them*?"

"It's not a question of a woman owing a man anything," said Kate, "but you have to face facts. Work it out for yourself. How is that switchboard girl benefitting the firm by leaving her fellow workers to do her work, while she's off skiving all the time? Or by tarting herself up in the ladies' cloakroom before she condescends to stroll into the office?"

"No benefit at all that I can see," said Kathy tersely.

"Exactly. And yet you say she's never criticised for her slapdash approach."

"No more she ain't," cried Kathy.

"If all things were equal, Kathy, she would be reprimanded every day, like you are—like I was. She's not because she's a different breed from us; she's judged by different rules. It won't change; it will always be you getting criticised; but she's Northern Hemisphere. She can ride over it; she knows she's safe whatever she chooses to do, or not to do. The fact is, we don't belong in their offices and never will do. Hand in your notice, Kathy. The job is making you ill."

"But I want the money," protested Kathy desperately. "I want to be independent; to 'ave a place of me own. I want new clothes an' to be able to treat meself now an' again. For Gawd's sake, Kate, can't you get that into your 'ead?"

Kate was quiet for a moment, as she recognised in her naive young friend's anguish, her own crushed aspirations, all too obviously duplicated here. She too was poor and weary; insecure and unhappy, and would have welcomed a little money and stability with open arms. A regular income would have ended the obligation to live under the same roof as her aunt in Terminal Lane; she could have discovered the pleasure of owning a dwelling of her own. Like Kathy, she would have liked more than anything in the world to hold up her head proudly, and support herself; but she realised that working in the offices of the Northern Hemisphere was no solution. Tears welled up in her eyes, and at last she cried out:

"Oh, Kathy! You're only seventeen years old, but already you look so drawn and tired. You were so happy-go-lucky; so full of life before you went to work in the Northern Hemisphere. I'd have given anything to have been like you were then, before those office cut-throats got to you. Are they treating you so cruelly? I think they must be. Oh, it's criminal; downright murderous!"

Kathy got to her feet abruptly and prowled about, her gaze unfixed. "Yes," she hissed, "it *is* bleedin' murderous, but I ain't the forgivin', passive type. I tell you now: I'm goin' to do somethin' about all the stick I'm gettin' 'urled at me!"

Kate forgot her tears on hearing her threatening tone. "What do you mean, Kathy? What are you going to do?"

"I don't know yet," seethed the younger woman, "but I'll think of somethin'." And she stormed out into the passage and out of the house.

Kate sat on despairingly, the untouched supper lying on the table before her. She did not need to rise to know that Kathy had gone. How she longed to guide her to some happier path. Poor girl, she thought; she seemed to be in the grip of a tragedy which was remorselessly unfolding.

Chapter Eighteen

"I'll be 'avin' two slices of bread if you're cuttin' any," said Aunt Nancy to Kate, hardly pausing as she made her way into the drawing room to eat her breakfast.

Kate stood, irresolutely clutching the bread knife, the cast of the previous night's dreams—which had been disturbed—still heavy on her. She shook herself in a vain effort to clear her head and began firmly to slice. But she was careless; in her distracted state she managed to nick the end of her forefinger with the sharp blade. Instantly, the blood welled and spattered on the board; she hurried to the sink to bathe the wound under the tap. Then she had to search for a strip of waterproof plaster.

"Are you all right in there, Kate?" called Aunt Nancy. "I'm still waiting for me two slices."

"I cut myself with the bread knife," replied Kate; her aunt came bursting in.

"You go about daydreamin' too much, young lady," she reproved her as soon as she saw it was not serious. "Oh, give it 'ere then," she added, taking the loaf and efficiently detaching a few slices. The knife was left by the sink and both went to finish their breakfasts in the front room.

Later, Aunt Nancy went up as usual to have her bath, her flip-flops slapping on every step of the shabby stairs. The water system rumbled overhead; hot and cold mixed, battered the stained enamelled bath into which they poured.

But Kate, standing in the passage, was soon disturbed by another noise. Turning to the front door, she was startled to see the wild shape of a head moving beyond the frosted glass half panel. The visitor struck again on the door another resounding blow, but before this could be repeated or more damage done, Kate drew back the bolts and opened the door to see who it was. Imagine her shock and dismay when the staring, unkempt creature outside shuffled forward.

"I'm fed up!" it roared. "They keep givin' me work which I ain't been trained for; an' then blamin' me when I end up makin' a mess of it! They tell me I'm useless; sometimes they just make me sit at me desk doin' nothin'—sod all for the rest of the bleedin' day!"

"Kathy!" cried Kate in surprise. "Aren't you a bit early? It's only ten o'clock. Or have you got a day off today?"

"Then that switchboard girl, that slut!" continued Kathy in heedless vehemence. "'er and that nasty, gosspin' clerk gang up on me tellin' me to bring in a book to read, or do some knittin' or sewin'. 'Ain't you got anythin' to occupy your mind?' they keep asking. "Well, I *ain't* there to occupy me mind! I want work to do, but they won't bleedin' give it to me! And if I *do* pick up a magazine because I'm bored out of me skull, that bitch of a supervisor pounces and tells me I'm wastin' company time. She's a right fat cow, she is. You should see 'er, Kate. She sits there stuffin' 'er face all day, and then 'as the nerve to say she 'as a manfriend! A right Northern 'Emisphere slag!"

Kate's heart was moved to pity when she saw how haggard her young friend had become. It was all the more obvious when, in an unguarded moment, Kathy pushed away the disorder of her hair from her face. There were bags under her eyes which looked as if they had been injected with some monstrous black dye. The corners of her delicate mouth were perpetually turned down; her clear forehead was now puckered; her eyes themselves were fevered and seemed ready to start out of her head!

Kate knew that for weeks she had been treading that invisible frontier, beyond which lies an unknowable land full of howling and pain and disorientation. There is no peace to be found there; it is no refuge; but sometimes—when the mind is driven too hard, when the pressures can no longer be faced—the harassed soul sidesteps that way, and is lost. Kathy was that driven, harassed and lost soul.

Kate reached out gently to take her hand. "Kathy," she said softly, "sit down. Listen: I've told my mother all about you in the numerous letters I have written. I'm sure she would love to meet you. Why don't you come with me to the International Olympics at the end of this month? Bruce is taking me. Mother will be there, and Rebecca—you'd like her—and Deborah, who is such a kindly soul. We could sit in the stand and watch the athletes, and have a few days off. Go on, say you'll come!"

"No, Kate," Kathy grunted irritably. "Out of the question. I can't go."

"Why can't you go?" asked Kate, frowning.

"I won't!" cried the girl. "Don't try to force me; I'd be too frightened!"

"Kathy, dear Kathy, why should you be frightened of going to the Olympics?" Kate felt the tears coming; she forced them back.

"When I get there I might suddenly collapse; then I'd be so ill I'd never be able to come 'ome."

"No, you won't," Kate assured her. "Besides, we'll all be with you to look after you."

"You wouldn't, you know. You wouldn't be able to get me back in one piece, 'cause I'd disintegrate."

"Now, Kathy," said Kate a little more firmly, "you're not making any sense; you're not well. What does your mother have to say about this? Surely she can see how upset you are?"

"Me mum?" Kathy replied scornfully. "What the 'ell does *she* care, as long as I bring in the money? It's all gone wrong, Kate," she continued hoarsely. "Supervisor's told me I ain't goin' to pass me six months' probationary—and I ain't been there more than two months. She says she won't give me work because she can see I can't cope. 'Ow does she know, if she doesn't give me a chance? She also says that the men don't like me. Surprise, surprise! Like me enough to rape me, didn't they, all those years ago? I'm beat, Kate; they've got me. I've been chewed up and sucked dry. Oh, 'ell, I feel so ill!"

Ill Kathy indeed looked; ill, and worn, and sickened by the world she saw about her. If that was all it was, it was bad enough; but Kate feared there was worse behind.

She rose tentatively from the sofa on which they had both been sitting. "Kathy," she said, "let me take you to a doctor. I'm sure they could help."

Kathy shook her head; she was hardly listening.

"Kate," she said, rising also, "whatever opinions I may have of the 'uman race, don't think I ain't still fond of you. They're all rats out there, but you're different. I'd like to kill every one of them," she ranted, "stab 'em through the heart: all those greasy businessmen and their wives. It wouldn't 'urt 'em, because you know, they've got no feelings. They don't feel a thing. Funny, isn't it?" Then, as if with an immense effort, she clawed her way back to sanity. "I've got something for you, Kate." She drew an object out of her pocket and came closer, holding it concealed in her clenched fist. "This is to show 'ow I trust you, Kate. Close your eyes."

Kate obeyed, though it frightened her to do so. She was not sure what Kathy would do next, so disturbed did she seem. But she feared even more what her friend's reaction might be if she were caught peeping. As she waited, she sensed that Kathy had moved away from her; then there was the faint sound of scraping metal from the kitchen which made her blood run cold.

"Kathy?" she called a few moments later. "Where are you, Kathy?"

"You can open your eyes now," said the girl, her voice sounding close by.

Kate did so with relief, to find her friend standing in the place where she was before, with one hand held out, the other concealed behind her back. In the open palm extended towards her, lay a small round box.

"I want you to keep this as somethin' to remember me by," she said, as Kate lifted the lid to find a golden, heart-shaped locket reposing on a velvet nest inside. "Open it, Kate. I bought it with most of me last week's wages."

Kate applied her thumbnail to the side of the locket and its lid sprang up to reveal a charming photograph of Kathy, as she had looked no more than a month or two earlier, before bitterness had etched her face; while the light of hope still shone in her eyes. The present was so unexpected, and the contrast with Kathy's present state so poignant that she had to turn away as the tears threatened to swamp her eyes. She wiped them off her cheeks and bit her lip, and swung round again to thank the dear child for such a beautiful gift.

But Kathy had fled. Kate caught just a glimpse of her shabby green dress in the passage outside; then she heard the front door crash open. Racing there, she found it swinging idly. Outside in the squalid lane, one or two people were moving slowly along, but of Kathy Fellowes there was no trace.

Chapter Nineteen

The vast Amphitheatre was slowly filling up; the yellow stolas of those Eastern Hemisphere inhabitants who had already taken their seats made brilliant blots of colour on the terraces.

"Where did your mother say we should meet?" asked Bruce as he and Kate advanced down the broad gangway; Aunt Nancy following busily behind.

"In the third row of the Arena," replied Kate. "By the second entrance."

"'Ave you two got the tickets?" said Aunt Nancy, in her usual bustling manner, "or 'ave you lost them on the way?"

"It's all right, Miss Brannigan," Bruce told her firmly, "I have them here in my wallet. I very rarely mislay what I'm supposed to keep. One of the advantages, you might say, of being an insurance representative."

"All right, young man," said Aunt Nancy, drawing herself up. "There's no need to go on about your efficiency; I think I've got the message. Oh, Kate," she added, changing the subject, "that kitchen knife I saw you tryin' to slice the bread with the other week; the one with the wooden 'andle. It's missin'. I can't find it anywhere."

"I haven't used it since, Aunt Nancy," Kate replied innocently. "In fact, I can't even remember putting it back in the drawer."

"Daydreamin' again, were we, Kate?" said Aunt Nancy petulantly, adjusting the string of her broad-brimmed hat. "You'll forget where you put your head one of these fine days. Well, until you remember, I suppose we're going to have to manage without it."

But her aunt's irritation was no more than a distant buzzing in Kate's ears. It was such a beautiful day, and the spectacle and the grandeur of the occasion were so refreshing that it seemed pointless to concern herself with trifles. From the loudspeakers boomed the patriotic music that was bound to stir all hearts. How she loved the Olympics; partly because this annual event was the only occasion on which all inhabitants from the five quarters of the country were allowed to sit together undisguised, in their traditional, customary attires. It also gave her a sort of thrilled, nostalgic pleasure to watch the tournaments of archery and Karate, those two sports which she had used to practise. Indeed, the entire atmosphere of the occasion was relaxed—except in one particular. There was a separate, mini arena, called 'The Pit', which lay deep underground for those 'down and outs' who chose to watch the Pankration tournament; no self-respecting Hemisphere inhabitant would patronise this, as it was considered 'nasty and low.'

There was still no sign of the other members of the party. Bruce was all for returning to the main entrance in case they had confused the instructions, but nothing had yet been decided when two middle-aged Northern Hemisphere women, smartly dressed in tweed two-piece suits and court shoes plumped down on seats near to where Kate stood.

For the next few moments they sat there, refined and contained, eyeing everybody within their field of vision, like two hawkish scrutineers. Immediately after, a young Non-Hemisphere woman passed, on her way to the Pankration tournament. She was a voluptuous creature of about nineteen or twenty, with long blonde hair and a curvaceous figure which even her dowdy Non-Hemisphere attire was unable to conceal. Those assets, however, were not what attracted the ladies' attention, for she was also decked out in priceless, sparkling jewels. The incongruity fascinated Kate, too, but it was the two spinsters who spoke.

"Oh, look," said one, "it's one of those whores. She has the nerve to show her face at an event like this!"

"She's not stopping, thank goodness," commented the other. "She seems to know her place. What a scandal if she were to sit up on the terraces!"

"I've read about those brothels in the papers," said the first. "They're underground, too, apparently. Such animals! Didn't she look pleased with herself, though? Did you notice? Selling their bodies is one job that Non-Hemispheres seem able to hold down, ha, ha!"

Then some other object caught their eye.

Kate was distracted by a tap on the shoulder. She turned round to see her mother, with Deborah and Rebecca standing cheerfully at her side.

"Kate," she said reservedly, "we're here at last. I do hope you haven't been waiting long. Hello, Nancy," she added, turning aside to greet Kate's aunt.

"Hello, Kate," said Deborah warmly. "Lovely to see you again. What a beautiful locket you have on!" she exclaimed, staring with fascination at the golden pendant which Kate was wearing round her neck.

"Thank you, Deborah," said Kate. "It was a present from a friend of mine who, unfortunately, was unable to make it to the Olympics today."

"Oh, what a shame!"

"Yes, she's not very well."

"Oh dear! I hope she gets better soon."

"Kate!" Now it was Rebecca's turn to come forward. Kate had to control an instinctive urge to draw back. "Hello there! Ages since we last met! I'm so glad you're coming to my wedding."

"Oh, Rebecca," said Kate half-heartedly. "I'm looking forward to it."

"So am I!" replied the young woman with excited enthusiasm. "Roll on the 2nd of May!"

"This is Bruce, everyone," said Kate timidly, as Bruce politely shook the hands of each Eastern Hemisphere woman in turn. "Bruce, this is my mother, Miriam; her neighbour, Deborah; and my friend, Rebecca."

"My! What a handsome couple you make!" cried Deborah. "Like Rebecca and Judah! I hope you two will be naming the day pretty soon?"

"Oh, I expect we shall," Bruce assured her complacently; but Aunt Nancy gave a heavy drawling cough. Fortunately, at that moment, the music from the loudspeakers gave way to the shrilling of trumpets, indicating that the tournament was about to commence; and Aunt Nancy's energy was diverted to directing everyone to their seats.

Kate sat down tensely, with the thought nagging at her that it was her duty to inform her mother that Bruce was a married man; if she was not careful, Aunt Nancy would feel obliged to spill the beans herself. But Kate's courage was not up to facing the ordeal that day. She would put it off until Rebecca's wedding, she decided; for all along she had intended that the revelation should be spoken, rather than coldly sealed in a letter.

The first part of the martial arts tournament comprised Jiu-Jitsu and Aikido. With neither of these disciplines was Kate familiar, and therefore she did not watch with much interest. Bruce's attention, however, was rapt; she could see he was reliving his own former triumphs. Both events were won by Eastern Hemisphere entrants as usual; the crowd roared as they held up their trophies to be admired.

Next came the Karate, beginning with a number of not-too-sturdy women wearing green belts, gracefully performing Katas ranging from Keon to Heian Yondan Kata, leading up to the mauve belt stage. Here, Kate sat up and began to take notice. Then other women took their place, moving with precision and finely adjusted force—athletic combatants of the brown belt and finally the black belt grades, whose power and skill filled Kate with both envy and awe.

The male Olympic Karatekas came next; Kate leaning over towards Bruce, whom Aunt Nancy had placed out of harm's way on her left side.

"Fantastic display, isn't it?" she whispered, her eyes glowing.

"Not bad," conceded Bruce, "although I've seen better."

"Shhh!" hissed Aunt Nancy, asserting herself. This ain't the time nor the place for conversation!" Whereupon they both lapsed back into silence.

The women Karatekas' free-fighting tournament was fast and furious; Kate watched it with a child-like fascination, marvelling at the exhibition of such strength and courage. The victor was a rather massive Eastern Hemisphere Swede who was presented with a trophy in the form of a golden disc, and a bright yellow stripe which would be stitched to her ji in permanent recognition of her achievement.

The men's free-fighting tournament was even more ebullient, and Kate sat uneasily, wondering if Bruce had been as fierce a combatant in his days as an Olympic competitor. She searched his face for some sign of his involvement, as the fighters dealt their heavy blows; but he appeared unmoved; that handsome, inscrutable mask of his made her fear him a little.

The winning contestant was a tall, Eastern Hemisphere Briton. He received a lengthy, standing ovation from the crowd, which he seemed to accept as his right, raising his golden disc and stripe as a conductor might his baton. The sweat trickled abundantly down the streak of gold cosmetic which ran across his tanned cheek to represent his victorious native quarter.

Then at last the teams withdrew from the Arena, the trumpets sounded to indicate that this part of the contest was at an end, and Kate, consulting her programme, discovered that there would be an interval of two hours before the archery and biathlon tournaments took place.

She felt a touch of a familiar hand on her wrist, and Bruce eased her up from her seat, leading her aside with him into the gangway.

"Come back with me to the Northern Hemisphere this evening when this is all over," he whispered gently in her ear. "Marjatta's taken Lenni away to visit relatives in Finland for the weekend. We'll have the house to ourselves."

Before Kate could answer, Aunt Nancy, in her self-appointed role as chaperone, had joined them and was looking eagerly from one to the other.

"Whispering? Whispering?" she said, her eyes as sharp as a bird's.

"It was nothing, Aunt Nancy," said Kate, evading her gaze.

"Don't look like it either," came the sarcastic response. "Anyway, we'd best get a move on. Your mother will be waiting for us in the seventh row."

Kate swallowed hard as, with the rest of the party, she made her way to the restaurant of the Amphitheatre. Questions were shot at her, to which she gave mechanical replies. She tried to be attentive and relaxed, but inwardly she was in a state of wild panic. She knew what Bruce had just intimated; it was written in his eyes. Horrifying images from the distant past sprang up to haunt her; in her mind she found herself repeating: "I'm not ready!"

As she sat down at the table, she entered her own private prison.

Chapter Twenty

The sun was down, the moon was slyly peeping. Having detached Kate from her aunt, Bruce was guiding her to the platform of the Electro-Train. He had told Kate that his home was a minute's walk from the Electro-Terminus, and she, still searching desperately for a way out, had replied that it was as well: it meant that she could get home in reasonable time.

"That's not what I had in mind," said Bruce firmly, as they seated themselves on one of the platform's plastic benches. "You can stay at my house overnight. I'll take you back to your aunt's place in the morning."

Kate heard his crude proposal, and let her hand remain in his, though she could not repress the inward shudder. Her eyes were fixed on the long electric cable which was in mild spasm as the Electro-Train approached. Anything was better than discussing, or even referring to what she feared so much. She stumbled as they entered the nearest carriage, and Bruce had to catch hold of her arm.

"Are you tired, Kate?" he asked.

"No," she mumbled. "I don't think it's that."

They took their seats and the Electro-Train sped on soundlessly, slicing through a landscape which was fading in the dusk.

"You're not unwell, I hope?"

Kate felt convulsed, eaten up; how she hated all this probing! She shook her head quickly and stared out of the window, not seeing anything. But when they reached his station, and they were speeding down in the communal lift, she felt impelled to say:

"I . . . I'm a bit frightened, that's all."

"Don't be afraid, Kate," he assured her. "I'll be gentle with you; trust me."

She glanced at her watch; but more vivid in her mind's eye was a crushed and mangled timepiece of long ago, lying in the Farmlands' dust. This superimposition alarmed her even more. Then she heard Bruce laugh, and his laughter had a hateful, unnatural sound, as if it were some stranger at her side, whose arm was locked with hers, and who was hurrying her forward.

"What's the matter?" she asked, almost truculently.

"You're so tense, Kate," he told her, "but you're very sweet. Don't you ever look at yourself in a mirror? Don't you like what you see?"

"A mirror is not oneself," retorted Kate, momentarily forgetting her fear. "Mirrors only reflect nasty, external rubbish."

"What's the matter? You're as jumpy as a cat, Kate. What are you afraid of, love?"

She suppressed a groan of irritation and merely asked how much further it was. They were walking through a wretched dark alley which seemed to magnify her fears. If they could have parted there and then—he to take his way and she to take hers—she would have sighed with relief. But she had to grit her teeth and go on.

"It's all right, Kate," he said, pausing briefly to take her hand. "I realise by the way you're reacting that this will be your first time. I'll take care of you. It'll be fine, you'll see."

"I want to be away from this dreadful alley," she said breathlessly, haunted by her memories.

"You will be very soon," he assured her. "It's only a few more steps up here."

They hurried on their way. Kate's spirits remained oppressed by her unspoken fears. It seemed important, for some reason that she could not explain, not to look directly into Bruce's face. She let him guide her, keeping her eyes down, the night menacing her with its blocks of darkness and rustling shapes. Even breathing seemed difficult to her; as if a giant hand were pressing on her, with some evil intent.

She waited on the doorstep of a house which, in the only glance she gave it, had a shabby, unprepossessing appearance. Bruce was excited and was finding difficulty fitting his key into the lock. He succeeded at last and threw the door open, going ahead to turn on the light in a wide, luxurious hall. Kate noticed pictures of vast Finnish landscapes on the walls.

Taking her arm firmly, he led her up the plushly carpeted stairs. He was merciless; he would allow her no escape.

"This is the bedroom," she heard him say.

In her head, the voice said louder and louder: "I don't want this! I don't want this!"

His fingers were awkward and heavy as she felt him slowly unbutton her mac. He eased her dress from her body, and she stood inert in the cold moonlight, still evading his eyes.

"Look at me, Kate," he said gently, tilting her head with his fingertips under her chin. "This is not a punishment, you know. I realise that you were attacked in the past, and I want to help you to overcome it. Why do you look away from me, Kate?"

Then she had to yield to his brute insistence and gaze into his eyes—for the first time since they had left the crowded Amphitheatre. And the man she saw there was not the athletic Bruce; this was another man's face, seen once before and never quite forgotten. It destroyed her when she realised who it was. This face had a motive to ruin; this face had reappeared to do her harm; she felt that very clearly.

Now that she looked, she could see it in every detail. Its hair was black and greasy, brushed tightly behind its ears. It had thick, rubbery lips and hostile, deep-set eyes. It was tall and came from the Farmlands. It had done its foul business ten years ago, and at this crisis point it had returned to make sure that it held her still.

Shrinking back in fear and alarm, she fell across the bed, guarding with all her strength the lacy undergarment which still covered her nakedness. Bruce pursued her on hands and knees. In stark terror, she snatched up her mac, freed herself from him and fled into another room.

Here, too, through the un-curtained windows, the moonlight spread over floor and wall, like drifted snow. It drifted over her, too, and whitened her red mac as she worked desperately to push her arms into it, and button it up.

The heavy vengeful sounds of footsteps came outside the door. The door flew back with a crash, and Bruce walked in holding her crumpled, Non-Hemisphere dress. Seeing her expression, he flung it at her in scorn.

"You shouldn't have run away, Kate. Why don't you trust me?" He sounded angry and frustrated. "I'd have been gentle with you just now if you'd allowed us to take our relationship further."

Kate did not reply. What was she to say? How could she possibly explain that another, a ghostly third had been present at their lovemaking; a vile destroyer.

"It's a great shame," he went on furiously. "You've the looks most women would envy, but what's the use? You won't let a man get near you. Look, I know you were attacked ten years ago. But that's a long, long time; time heals all wounds."

She showed him the scar on her wrist. "But the scars remain, Bruce," she said. "I wish they didn't, but they do."

"Perhaps that's because it's what you secretly want," he retorted in disgust. "Perhaps you don't love me, after all. Perhaps you're merely using your past attack as an excuse because you don't want a full relationship."

"That's not true!" she cried. "I *do* love you, Bruce."

"You mean platonically," he sneered. "Like a brother?"

"No," she said earnestly, "that's not it at all. I'm extremely attracted to you. I don't merely see you as a day-to-day friend. You send me further than that."

"Then why can't you make love to me? Why do you repel my advances if I mean something to you? How can I believe you when you say you're attracted to me when you are doing nothing to prove it?"

Kate stared at him forlornly, not knowing how to reply. He grew impatient and demanded an answer. She did her feeble best.

"When we were in the bedroom just now," she began lamely, "I couldn't see you. I kept seeing someone else. He was my attacker—I was horrified!"

He gave her a wry look. "I'm sorry, Kate, but I don't believe you."

"What . . . what does *that* mean?"

"It means goodbye, Kate." His voice was as expressionless as his face. "I think it would be best if we both called it a day."

She ran from that house, still clutching her Non-Hemisphere dress in her hand. Her eyes blinded with tears, she made her way back to the familiar squalor of Terminal Lane, via the labyrinth, without caring if it would lead her into another brutal attack.

Chapter Twenty-One

The whole setting was familiar to her from childhood; the majestic Rubicon temple; the adjacent forum and basilica; the public baths where her father had offered to instruct her in self-defence; the high Amphitheatre which lay beyond the wall surrounding the town; the watchtowers and ditches and the vigilantly guarded gate, through which she, now a foreigner, humbly made her way.

With her wedding gift for Rebecca held under her arm, she hung about the entrance to the temple, feeling too self-conscious to go in alone. She had decided this, and was looking around for her mother and Deborah, when she spotted a vaguely familiar couple drawing near. She realised, as they came closer, that they were Rebecca's parents, whom she had often spoken to years ago when she was a regular visitor at their village to see Rebecca. She turned, therefore, to wave to them, but on seeing her they threw her a cagey, sidelong glance and hurried inside. Kate's smile of welcome faded and a cloud seemed to run before the sun.

"Hello, Kate! Here we are again!" said a cheery voice. Kate swung round to find Deborah, who had just arrived with her mother.

"Hello, Kate," said Mrs Tiberius more distantly. "How's Aunt Nancy?"

"Oh, she's fine," replied Kate. "Taking everything in her stride as usual."

Mrs Tiberius lowered her voice. "She said something to me at the International Olympics. I gather there is a topic which you and I need to discuss."

"Did she tell you what it concerned?" asked Kate, who had a pretty good idea.

"No, but she did say it was only right that I should be informed. In fact, she was most insistent."

"Yes, I'm sure she was," replied Kate acidly. "Well, Mother, this is hardly the time nor the place, would you say?"

"If we're to get a good seat, I do think we ought to go inside," Deborah diplomatically suggested. "People are arriving all the time; it would be nice to be near the front."

"Yes," agreed Kate, "let's go in. I'm sure it will be a fantastic wedding."

The temple was huge, but the congregation was also a large one. Most of the people, after this space of time, were unknown to Kate, although she did notice Rebecca's mother inconspicuously sitting two rows behind an elderly Eastern Hemisphere couple. As the watchtower struck noon, all rose to their feet; the Wedding March struck up and Kate felt her heart flutter when she saw Rebecca gracefully gliding down the aisle, arm in arm with her father; her white, sequined veil trailing along the patterned floor. She looked at ease with herself, her head prettily adorned with orange, fragrant blossoms, a bouquet of peonies and gladioli lightly held in one hand. By the altar a more nervous Judah stood waiting for her.

The service was led by a tall, young clergyman from the Southern Hemisphere Synod, wearing purple robes. All proceeded without incident; the vows were exchanged and the rings, and the young couple were leaving the church when something behind the altar caught Kate's eye.

"Kate, where are you going?" exclaimed her mother, as her daughter climbed the marble steps to take a closer look. Without so much as a reply, she advanced towards the window, where a man in full armour stood beckoning her. In his right hand he held a pilum; in his left, a little wooden bowl that she had seen somewhere before.

"Can I help you? Are you lost?" she asked him, as a feeling of intimacy invaded her senses. The conversation had got no further when Mrs Tiberius came up.

"Kate, what are you doing?"

"That man by the window," she replied, half turning, her eyes filled with tears. "He wanted to speak to me."

"What man?"

Kate turned back towards the stained glass window expectantly, but all was different there; the armed soldier was now nowhere to be seen. It was a moment of vision; she knew it had been her father.

"Do come along, Kate!" said her mother, with a touch of irritation. "This is no time for silly games."

Kate did not reply. The last members of the congregation were leaving the temple by the doors at the far end. She descended the altar steps.

"Kate," went on Mrs Tiberius, "we may not get another chance to be alone, so I do think it only fair that you tell me what it is that your aunt has been hinting at. I am your mother; I do have a right to know."

"Did she point you in any particular direction?" asked Kate sourly, cursing the meddlesome creature in her mind.

"She did not go into any details," replied Mrs Tiberius, "but I'm almost certain it involves the man you are courting."

"Oh, Bruce!" murmured Kate in an offhand way. "You liked him, didn't You, Mother? But I never got around to mentioning that he's a married man with a four-year-old daughter. Aunt Nancy didn't approve of that!"

Mrs Tiberius was shocked. Her eyebrows shot up.

"Neither do I approve of it!" she said severely. "This puts a completely different light on the situation. Here have I been telling everyone how happy I am that you have found a partner at last, and that there was a good chance of your getting married, when all along you knew it was out of the question! It was very wrong of you, Kate, not to tell me about it!"

"Oh well, you needn't worry any more about that, either," the young woman retorted. "You see, the relationship between myself and Bruce no longer exists. He sent me packing at the beginning of last month. He no longer wants me."

"Goodness, Kate! Whatever happened for him to reject you like that?" Her mother was looking more and more surprised.

"I'm sexually inadequate, Mother," said Kate calmly. "I was unable to please him when the time came. Is that enough for you, or do you want me to go into the details?"

"Kate, Kate!" her mother reproached her. "I realise you must be disappointed at how it has turned out, but there's no need to go off the rails like that while explaining the situation to me, especially in a place of worship! You're very frank, Kate."

"I'm absolutely fed up, Mother," replied Kate almost truculently. "I've had to put up with a lot over the past ten years and I'm just about sick of it; and if anyone doesn't think that the attack I suffered ten years ago was not enough to put me off men for the rest of my life, well, that's their problem, and not mine!"

"Now then, Kate," said her mother, beginning to walk in her agitation. "That will be enough of that. We'll consider the matter closed."

"Oh, I agree!" snapped Kate, unrelenting. "The fact is that I'm frigid, whether Bruce is married or not."

They joined the guests in the basilica next door without another word.

Rebecca, of course, was there, looking radiant in her dress of sequined lace, and chatting convivially. As soon as she saw Kate she came hurrying forward, drawing Judah—who had been having an amusing conversation with the good-natured Deborah—along with her.

"Oh, Kate, I'm so glad you could make it!" she said joyously, taking her in her arms. "How very very nice! May I introduce you to my husband, Judah? He's heard so much about you."

"How do you do, Kate?" said the young man, beaming and shaking her hand.

"Nice to meet you," murmured Kate. Her tone was aloof and reserved. She had been intending to tell them how pleased she was for them, and what a happy day it must be. But suddenly, standing alone, without a man of her own, she felt resentful; the words obstinately refused to come.

"Mrs Tiberius!" called Rebecca, as she saw Kate's mother advance, slowly and gracefully, towards her. "How lovely to see you!"

Kate, silent and uneasy, was a bystander at the exchange of courtesies which followed. She heard her mother say rallyingly: "Well, aren't you going to congratulate the bride and groom, Kate?"

"Oh—congratulations, Rebecca and Judah," she rapped out automatically. She could do no more. "Excuse me for a minute," she added, and she hurried from the place to seek solace in the quiet of the deserted forum. On the first steps she found, she sat down disconsolately, cupping her face in her hands. The wind blew and she heard the laughter of the guests from a distance.

Presently, a light hand rested on her shoulder, and she looked up into Deborah's kind face. The woman came to sit down beside her.

"What's the matter, Kate?" she asked gently. "I saw the look on your face when you left the basilica just now. Is there something troubling you, by any chance?"

"Yes," blurted Kate from the depths of her despair. "As a matter of fact there is."

"Do you want to talk about it?"

"I'm afraid it's not that easy to explain."

"What is it? You know it's better not to bottle things up. Tell me: I may be able to help."

Kate sighed and stared into the distance. "I suppose," she began quietly, "it must have seemed rude of me not to have congratulated the bride and groom on their wedding, and to have practically fled from the reception the way I did; but the fact is I couldn't help it. When I saw them both standing there, looking so adult and sophisticated—Rebecca outshining everyone in her lovely, sequined dress—I felt so insignificant, so stupid! I felt as if I've been left a thousand years behind."

"But no two people's lives are ever the same," said Deborah soothingly. "You're a person in your own right, just as much as Rebecca is. You're just living a different life from her, that's all."

Kate shot her a bitter glance. "Yes, that's right. I am, indeed, living a very different life from my privileged friend and I resent that fact; I loathe it!"

"You shouldn't be so hard on yourself, Kate," said Deborah, placing a comforting hand on her arm. "You're a very beautiful young woman. There's no need for you to feel outclassed by Rebecca."

"Yes, I have to admit, I *am* jealous of her," burst out Kate. "Sounds good, doesn't it? Jealous of my own best friend, who invites me to her wedding, and is so welcoming. In fact, I'm so jealous I almost feel I hate her." She saw Deborah raise her eyebrows in surprise, but she pressed on. "I suppose when you reach a certain age, and you still have no partner of your own, and you see your friend happy with her partner, it's bound to have an effect. You begin to feel an obstacle; the odd one out; the misfit who tags along behind like a shadow, with no one or nothing to your name. There are Rebecca and Judah, with good jobs and a villa to move into; and here am I with nothing at all. It's as if I don't even exist."

"But you have Bruce," Deborah reminded her with a sympathetic smile.

Kate winced at the mere mention of the man.

"No," she muttered, "that's where you're wrong. I don't have Bruce. He rejected me when the physical side of our relationship didn't work out. Besides, he's married. What a mess, don't you agree?"

"Oh, Kate," said Deborah earnestly, "I'm so sorry. I had no idea."

"It doesn't matter. I can't face telling anyone about it—Aunt Nancy knows, of course, but then she's always poking her nose into everything. Actually, that's not the only thing," she continued on a sudden impulse. "There's something else—something which even Aunt Nancy doesn't know about."

Deborah, who noticed that she was not as cut up about Bruce as might have been expected, asked her what it was.

"Something's happened to my friend, Kathy."

"Good heavens! What's wrong with her?"

"I don't know exactly." Kate felt a great weariness stealing over her as she spoke. "All I know is that she's ill in some way. She . . . sometimes she doesn't make sense. She gets depressed easily. I wanted her to come with me to the International Olympics in March, but she was too scared; I think she was afraid she might not be able to get home again. I feel responsible for her, and yet I can't make her take my advice. Oh, Deborah, it's so nice of you to be so understanding. What with Kathy, and Bruce, and the fact that Rebecca and I have grown light years apart from each other, I don't know. I just don't know . . ."

She rubbed her forehead. She was thinking of that vision of her father, which she had seen less than half an hour before. If she were to mention that to Deborah, the good woman would undoubtedly think she was mad—but it had been so real. Deborah was right; voicing her worries had helped to lance the boil of agony.

"Things will sort themselves out, Kate, believe me," said Deborah as they stood together. "Now, let's go back inside, shall we? Or they'll all be wondering where we have both got to."

Chapter Twenty-Two

"Now, come, young lady; buck your ideas up," said Aunt Nancy as her niece sat gloomily at the kitchen table. "It'll do you no good sittin' there feelin' sorry for yourself. It would be better if you took a walk now that the weather's gettin' warmer; stop you broodin' over that young man, who ain't worth broodin' over anyway." She ignored Kate's reproachful look and automatically raised her voice.

"I always told you he was no good! A decent sort of man don't two-time 'is wife an' then ditch 'is mistress because 'e can't 'ave 'is wicked way with 'er. That Bruce was only after your body, Kate, an' you know that as well as I do!"

Kate shut her eyes briefly. "Do you mind if we don't talk about it?" she said. "I think we've already said as much as there is possible to be said on that subject."

"What about Kathy?" asked the irrepressible Aunt Nancy. "'Ave you seen 'er lately?"

"No, I haven't. I think she spends a lot of her spare time at the lighthouse talking to the lighthouse keeper. She mentioned something about it a few months ago, just after she started work."

"A fine friend *she* turned out to be," Aunt Nancy remarked huffily. "She could be over 'ere consolin' you, instead of stuck up in some faraway light'ouse. It's a strange place to be spendin' one's time in, anyway. She couldn't be bothered to come to the Olympics two months ago, when we all went, I noticed. Fine, loyal folk *you* attract, Kate Brannigan. If I ever set eyes on either Kathy or Bruce again, you can be sure I'll give them a piece of my mind!"

Kate stood up apathetically, reflecting that Aunt Nancy would not recognise Kathy if she saw her. She felt lonely and utterly deserted; recently it had occurred to her to wonder if that was how her father had felt during the last few months before his death.

"I think you're right; I will take that walk, after all," she said, drifting out into the passage to fetch her mac from the cupboard under the stairs.

"The sooner you start acceptin' life the way it is, young lady, the better," Aunt Nancy officiously called after her.

Kate shut the door behind her and set off towards the labyrinth by way of the warm, sleepy shore. At this hour only a few listless vagrants were about, dead souls who never ventured into the Hemispheres. She thought of Bruce, and of the meals they had enjoyed in 'Politician's Square'. Memories of that happier time made her loss seem all the keener; she had some idle notion of revisiting the place as she stumbled down the steps into the warren.

As she walked on aimlessly, she came to a place which, in that underground world, she had never explored. A passage led off to it obscurely, and to other recesses of a similar kind where sexual congress occurred in areas set apart. It was a hidden place, but you knew you were getting close by the character of the obscenities drawn, scratched and painted on the surrounding walls. Here, wealth and jewels were exchanged for acts of darkness; sly men in city clothes went to have their choice of 'fallen' Non-Hemisphere women. Indeed, these underground caves formed a mini-quarter network of their own; as corruptively rich and prosperous as the Non-Hemisphere was barren and poor.

The temperature rose steadily as Kate approached. She, who had had no idea of going there, took off her mac under the impact of the heat. But a sudden gust of wind tugged it from her grasp, and with dismay she saw it being sucked down, far below into the verminous darkness of the sewers.

She paused, frowning, hoping for a contrary gust to return it to her. But this failed to happen and at last she was obliged to take a step in that direction. On it went fluttering before her, as if drawn by a compulsive force; she followed with the same dread as someone straying into the red, yawning mouth of a sleeping monster. The descent was something like a gullet, smooth and steepening; she began to be afraid that she would never emerge again; she resolved to abandon her mac and go no further.

Then she lost her footing and, colliding with the walls, went down willy nilly; she fell in a heap within feet of where her mac lay.

She stood up, not much hurt, and retrieved it. The fierce heat here was making her sweat; she was anxious to be gone. But round a bend just ahead, she saw the door that was the magnet for the lost souls who came here; it stood like a softly-glowing coal fire. The word '**Whorehouse**' was engraved in gigantic crimson letters above it, looking as if the rock itself was flesh and had received a brand. Rumours of voices and of an indefinable grating noise came from beyond the door; it was not quite closed and a ruttish perfume was wafting out.

In spite of herself, she stood irresolute, breathing in the scent of sexual abandon, strangely penetrated by a fume of incense and ripe green apples. It was lulling and hypnotic and she might have been overcome had the door not opened at that moment. A businessman in a blue, pin-striped suit, his face smeared with red lipstick, emerged amidst clouds of steam which spurted intermittently as if being released from the spout of a kettle. A young woman followed, decked in a garment of diamonds and crisp, rustling bank notes; a bitten apple dangled at her cleavage and played about her breasts as she ran. Both were laughing; they chased each other like children, but with lascivious intent. Then, catching his hand, the girl drew him back inside the whorehouse door.

Kate, half choked, turned in haste to make her way back to the main tunnel of the labyrinth. In the darkness, she felt a moist hand clasp its fingers round her wrist. She immediately tensed up, turning to face whoever her assailant might be. Instantly there was a blast of hot breath directed at her face, which loosened and relaxed her through her whole body.

In that moment she must have closed her eyes. When she opened them again, she saw a man standing before her with one hand raised, in which there glowed an immense diamond which seemed to gather into itself all that was purity and light. Fascinated by the abnormality of its size, she raised her baffled head to take a look at the person who held it. He was slim and handsome, with long, dark hair; he smiled at her wryly, directing her to look into the diamond again. She did so and, as he brought it closer to her face, she gasped to see within it the image of an enormous mansion with a swimming pool rippling gently in its back garden.

The man did not speak, but his eyes were eloquent, and they were fixed on her. He was tantalizing her with the world within the stone—her body for that unstressed, comfortable life. If she gave herself to him—and he was handsome and young—he implied that these things would be hers. Instead of poverty and aimlessness, he was promising wealth and splendour and a life apart.

So why did she hesitate—so little to lose for so much to gain? A rigid logic seemed to nullify the temptation; to her alert mind, the diamond-enclosed house was more securely locked than dead flies in amber. The perfection of its world was inviolate for it lay within a priceless diamond. One could not be reached unless the other were shattered; surely that forced entry would half destroy its value?

The handsome man seemed to read her mind, for his smile faded. He breathed on the gem and she saw the rippling water of the pool turn rigid with ice. Then, his eyes growing furious and black, he held up the stone and she watched it crumble instantly. With a cry, Kate turned and ran back to the main tunnel of the labyrinth.

Once she felt the cool air of the subway on her face again, she breathed a huge sigh of relief. Then she pursued her way more slowly to the cut-throat Northern Hemisphere, as she tried to make sense of the experiment in her mind. That she had been tempted was clear; even now it pained her to think of that beautiful stone ruthlessly reduced to dust.

But the tempter? As she emerged into the daylight at the end of the tunnel, all doubts faded. She had passed through the infernal kingdom. Though the handsome stranger had not come equipped with horns, or with a tail pushing through his clothes, she knew who he must be.

Chapter Twenty-Three

It was dark when Kate got home, dejected and worn out with wandering. Her aunt was nowhere about; taking off her mac, she flung it down, then went to help herself to a glass of Green Liquor from the cupboard above the cooker. As it flowed like a narcotic through her veins, the lids of her eyes felt heavy; the effort needed to keep them open could not match the ease with which they closed . . .

Rising from her chair, she glided noiselessly out into the lambent, evening landscape. From somewhere beyond the horizon a cold wind came howling, swirling Kate's dress and pressing it against her virginal curves. Beneath an incredible purple sky stretched a bed of frozen semen, edged by distant skyscrapers and the silently turbulent seas. Kate skated over the ice as the wind continued to whistle; a grey figure kept pace with her, its shadowy arm in hers. They halted when they reached the curved 'S' of 'Semen', the shrill wind growing fiercer. Kate crouched down in an attempt to break the ice with her fist. She managed it after several attempts, the serpentine curve becoming a narrow frith of rippling water. The grey figure stood motionless at her side, without a trace of emotion. A wedding veil of white lace and a bouquet of multi-coloured gladioli fell from the sky, and landed in the icy pool. She tried her utmost to retrieve it, but the bouquet was drawn under and was soon lost to sight, forever out of her reach.

The plain of semen ice grew lustrous and transparent, sucking Kate into another layer of landscape lying beneath it. She found herself standing on the beach on the fringes of the Non-Hemisphere. The labyrinth before her had been polished and renovated; but one part had somehow become detached and lay neglected on the rocks beyond. Through this ran Kathy, restored to her youthful beauty, an unbitten apple hanging about her neck. The sight brought Kate to tears; then Kathy disappeared and instead she saw Bruce, walking happily through the broken piece of tunnel wearing a bright yellow toga, a mini Finnish spruce tree held upright in his hand.

The sea beyond was choppy and turquoise as usual, but the lighthouse was different. It had become a glistening ivory tower, a kilometre in height. She found herself suddenly within its spotless, circular walls, sitting nonchalantly at a candlelit table; the indefinite grey figure occupying the seat opposite. Both held silver goblets in their hands and were drinking gallons of a thin alcohol; both, it seemed, were laughing uproariously . . .

A succession of heavy blows directed against the front door, woke her suddenly. Aching and wiping the sleep from her eyes, she trailed down the passage—and opened the door onto disillusion. After the radiant vision of her dream, the reality of Kathy's appearance was all the more appalling. Her breathing was laboured; her legs, face and hands were torn, there was a look of manic intensity in her eyes under the ploughed and knotted hair—all these were bad enough, but her dress was heavily marked with damp blotches which horribly resembled blood. Kate nearly threw up at the sight.

"I took your kitchen knife, Kate," whispered the monster through caked lips. "I just couldn't stand what I was goin' through no longer, so I went an' used it on somebody."

Kate's hair stood on end. "You mean you . . . ?" Kathy, you're having me on; you can't mean you . . . ?"

"Yes," groaned the girl. "I went an' stabbed someone—I killed the bitch 'an all!"

Kate found herself drawing back from this apparition. As she retreated into the house, so Kathy came forward, determined to divulge the full details of her crime.

"Well, I 'ad reason enough to do it," she continued. "She 'ad it comin' to 'er—the stupid, self-satisfied bitch!"

"Who?" asked Kate fearfully. "Who did you kill?"

"A business man's wife." Kathy shrugged. "'E was one of the men I worked for. She 'ad 'im round 'er little finger, an' 'e kept knockin' me an' praisin' 'er, till I decided I'd 'ad enough. It was 'Kathy, you've done this wrong'; Kathy, you're supposed to be dealin' with clients, an' you're not even makin' the effort to communicate with the people you work with'! 'E even called me into 'is room one day to give me a lecture on me attitude. But it was different when it came to 'is darling little Sheila! Oh yes, poor little Sheila, little porcelain girl—careful how you touch her in case you leave a fingermark! 'E'd ring 'er up from the office: 'Take care, Sheila,' 'e'd say. 'You can only do what you can do, Sheila.' The bastard! Well, she's got a few fingermarks over 'er now, as 'e'll find out this evening when 'e gets 'ome!"

"You've only just killed her?" asked Kate, her eyes widening in terror.

"What bloody difference does the time make?" shrieked Kathy. "The main thing is that I've done it. I've got rid of that annoyin', 'orrible bitch. What are you looking at me like that for, Kate? Can't you see what she was doin' to me? I was right, wasn't I?"

"But, but . . ." Kate stammered.

"I mightn't 'ave gone through with it, you know," continued Kathy, dropping into a conversational tone, "if somethin' 'adn't 'appened this mornin'. I told 'im I 'adn't bothered to take driving lessons because me reflexes were too slow; an' 'e goes an' gives me another lecture, doesn't 'e? Tells me I should be more positive an' that I shouldn't make excuses! Well, that was the final straw—when you think of 'is precious Sheila, sitting at 'ome doin' sod all! When was the last time *she* was positive? So that's 'ow it is, you see. Really, I 'ad no choice. There you are: they say it all comes right in the end."

Kate could feel her heart pounding; pity and fear worked together within her. For the first time in her life she wished that Aunt Nancy was there, so that she might not be so horribly exposed. Still Kathy talked on.

"I've lost weight again, Kate. Down to six stone now an' still droppin'. But I can't 'elp it, can I? The 'ole atmosphere of that office makes me feel sick. It's a nightmare; not as I imagined it would be like at all."

"But Kathy," Kate exclaimed fearfully, "you'll die!"

"Course I'll die!" screamed the girl, whose wizened face haunted her with its madness. "I know that. So did my father—I'll go like 'im. I blossomed out for nothin', didn't I? 'e bore me, 'e breathed life into me an' then 'e goes an' dies; lack of fuel; lack of fuel. All for nothin'!"

Kate just stared at her; but Kathy was not interested in hearing her replies.

"I've stopped comin' on each month," she said plaintively. "I don't bleed no more. Oh, you thought this was me, didn't you?" she continued, striking her stained front. "No, no, Kate, that's Sheila! I expect she's stopped bleedin' too, by now. Hubby will be disappointed when 'e gets 'ome. Oh no, no, no! What's the use of blossomin' out an' 'aving curves an' 'ips when you ain't goin' to 'ave no children, or no man 'oo's goin' to appreciate them?"

Suddenly she reached out and seized Kate by the wrist, exactly in the place where Satan had done. Kate nearly screamed, but desperately kept herself from doing so. From under the fog of her hair, Kathy's eyes blazed like someone looking at her from another world. She seemed unsexed, though mad with desire; cold, but burning up.

"I'm meltin' away, Kate; you won't be troubled with me much longer. You've been a good friend to me; I should have listened to you. Me and me mum were wrong. You were right about those Northern 'Emisphere offices. It's no place for the likes of us. So ugly—I'm so ugly! The men turn their eyes away; the bitches whisper be'ind me back. Well, I've given 'em somethin' to talk about now. Goodbye, Kate. Remember me—remember!"

"No, Kathy, wait!" Kate called after her, stirred from her torpor as the girl shuffled off down Terminal Lane. "Kathy, where are you going? What are you going to do?"

She sensed, however, that Kathy did not intend to be followed. She fled like a shadow to join the larger night. Kate, pausing only to pick up her mac, ran out after her into the empty street.

Chapter Twenty-Four

"Come along, now, look lively, you two," said the sergeant, trying to instil some backbone into the two police constables—a man and a woman—who trailed along behind him. "We haven't got all evening, you know. I know the Non-Hemisphere may not be your favourite assignment, but there's a job to be done, so come along!"

"I never knew such places still existed, Sarg," remarked the male constable, wrinkling up his face as they entered one of the less inviting streets of the contemptible Non-Hemisphere quarter.

"Oh, they exist all right, me lad," the sergeant told him. "It's just that, being relatively new to the job, you've yet to come across them. A perfect breeding ground for trouble, they are—thieving, rape, mayhem, you name it. It all happens here. You can't expect the standards of the Northern Hemisphere in this quarter. But we must do what we can. This is a very dangerous young woman. The sooner she's caught, the better."

The sleazy, ill-lit lane which the three Northern Hemisphere police officers had entered with such obvious reluctance was one of the most notorious in its neighbourhood. For this was Sugar House Lane, home to the most depraved elements of that verminous population. No sweet dreams or candies existed in Sugar House Lane. Behind its shattered facades were no decent families, struggling for respectability—parents who loved their children, diligent husbands or house-proud wives. 'Fencing' was the least violent pursuit in this dead-end 'city', where even police officers never went alone.

"Barking up the wrong tree, we are, in my opinion," said the young male constable uneasily, as they drew near the first house in the row. "This Fellowes woman won't be hiding out here. She'll be in the 'caves'; they say she's out of her mind."

"Nah, not her!" replied the female police officer. "I heard she had some sort of sexual problem. The last place to find her would be in a knocking shop."

"Now, shop bickering, you two," said the sergeant. "Be a bit more professional, can't you? Here, constable, I can't seem to raise anybody at this one. You have a go."

They had come to a halt in front of a filthy, tumbledown dwelling which it was difficult to imagine could be inhabited. It had a crazy leery appearance, like a drunk lying in his own vomit after a night on the town.

The sergeant had rapped on the peeling door panels without result; the constable, more enterprising, knelt down and shouted through the letterbox. This, like a stick thrust into a nest, seemed to have more effect, for presently the sound of movement could be heard from inside, and at last a coarse Non-Hemisphere voice could be heard grumbling:

"All right! All right! Give us a chance! I'm comin'!"

The door juddered open and a dishevelled young woman—who was probably in her early twenties, but in this quarter it was always difficult to be certain—dragged herself into sight. Her hair hung down in rat's tails, her face was filthy, her eyes bloodshot; she was holding together the rags of her dress across her protuberant stomach. She looked to be about six months' gone.

"Sorry to disturb you, missus," said the sergeant. "We were hoping you might be able to give us some help."

"Oh, Gawd help us, what 'elp can *I* give you or anyone?" moaned the wretched woman, her eyes going from one to the other of them. "'E ain't even in," she went on, before they had a chance to question her further. "An' I don't know when 'e's comin' back, so it's no good you waitin.'"

"This is not about your husband, missus," said the sergeant. "We're investigating a murder. May we come in for a few minutes?"

"Murder? Oh, my Gawd, my old man never done nothin' like that. You've come to the wrong 'ouse, you 'ave. It's 'er across the street you should go an' see. She could tell you a thing or two.—Eh, Doris?" she bawled suddenly, shuffling out onto the step and shaking her fist at a face that had appeared in a window opposite. "Asking about your 'usband!—Oh, all right, come in if you must," she continued in a quieter tone; and she led the way into a back kitchen that had to be seen to be believed. Dampness struck up from the ground; from the walls, strips of ancient paper hung forlornly. The table had one leg missing and was propped up on a box; an indescribable heap of rags which could once have been clothes, was piled on the floor by the stone sink with its wooden drainer. A cat, which had been helping itself to something from a basin on a chair, took one look at the visitors and leapt through the broken window into the ruined garden beyond.

"Murder, you say?" said the young woman, removing the basin from the chair and sitting down heavily; the officers remained standing. "'Oo is it this time?"

The sergeant cleared his throat. "We're investigating a Kathy Fellowes of Number 17 Gravel Lane, who had a job as a white-collar worker. She forced her way into the home of a young Northern Hemisphere businessman on Thursday night, and stabbed his wife to death in a frenzied, unprovoked attack. As the suspect is Non-Hemisphere, it's more than likely she's hiding in the vicinity, or you may perhaps have seen her."

"Well, she's not 'idin in 'ere," said the young woman defensively. "Kathy Fellowes? Never 'eard of 'er. What she look like, anyway? Can't tell if I've seen 'er, can I, if I don't know what she looks like."

The sergeant shot a glance at his two colleagues.

"Well, you see, missus, it's a bit difficult," he said. "According to some she's a young girl of about seventeen—slim, neatly dressed, medium height with long chestnut hair and green eyes."

"Yeah, yeah!" broke in the woman sarcastically, coughing and then clasping her stomach. "'Oo d'you think you're kiddin'? 'er livin' round 'ere? This is Sugar 'Ouse Lane, copper, not bleedin' Fancy Street."

"Other descriptions," went on the sergeant, "suggest a middle-aged woman, gaunt, with staring eyes, of a more—er, more tousled appearance."

"Make up your bleedin' mind. "Anyway, no: I ain't seen neither of them," said the woman defiantly.

"Then you've no objection if we search the house?"

"Oh, so you don't believe me, eh?" snapped the woman. "No—you search all you please, I don't care. Ain't nothin' 'ere, never 'as been. We ain't got nothin.'"

The sergeant made a signal to his two colleagues, who headed for the door.

"Only mind you don't rip up the beds, like that last lot did," she shouted after them. "Some people ain't got no respeck."

A silence fell as they listened to the sound of the two constables' boots on the boards of the room next door, and furniture being moved. The tap dripped incessantly into the sink, each splash adding to the green virulence on the wall behind. The woman sat with legs wide apart, head sunk, breathing asthmatically. The sergeant stood there awkwardly, his eyes swivelling to her when he heard her groan. She rubbed her bulging front.

Seeing him staring, she gave a grey smile.

"'E's startin' to kick, the little monkey," she said. "'E can't wait to be born. Fat lot of good it'll do 'im when 'e is. 'E don't know when 'e's well off. If 'e knew what was comin', 'e'd want to stay in there. Aw!" she groaned again. "Like 'is dad, always puttin' the boot in. You woke me up," she went on accusingly. "I was 'avin' a kip."

"Just as soon as the constables have finished," said the sergeant, "we'll be on our way."

"Yeah, all in a day's work for you, ain't it? As long as *you're* all right, sod everyone else!"

"While we're waiting," said the sergeant, ignoring her remark, "perhaps you could answer one last question. To your knowledge, have there been any previous reports of murders committed by Non-Hemisphere inhabitants upon inhabitants of the Northern Hemisphere? We like to keep our records up to date, you understand."

"You've got a bloody nerve!" the housewife almost shouted, her pain appearing to increase her sense of indignation. "I've already told you I don't know nothin'! Can't you get that into your 'eads! I'm stuck 'ere in this bleedin' 'ouse all day, while 'e's down the pub—what do I know about bleedin' murders?" She seemed driven to the edge of despair. "Ain't you got anythin' better to do than to 'arass a poor woman what's got another on the way after he went and did for the last one? Oh Gawd, will no one 'elp me? Oh, get out, get out!" She lifted her head to find the sergeant still looking at her inquiringly. "'Ow the 'ell should *I* know?" she roared.

The constables returned from their fruitless search, and the three officers took their leave.

Chapter Twenty-Five

Kate's first thought had been to go to the house in Gravel Lane. She found Mrs Fellowes in a state of near panic. Kathy had not come home, not even to collect her things, and she was terrified to think what could have happened to her. She was inclined to blame Kate, whom she had long seen as a rival influence; and even in her agitation she found no room for reconciliation there.

Sickened by this display, Kate had left her abruptly, without even saying goodbye, to continue her own searches in the quarter.

She was walking up Terminal Lane, looking out to sea despondently, and wondering where to look next, when her gaze fell on the solitary lighthouse. Suddenly it occurred to her that this was as likely a place as any other; she knew how Kathy had used to go there in the past; in her distracted state she could well have returned there, unthinkingly. Without considering the matter further, she made her way down to the shore.

The lighthouse stood far out on a rocky promontory, a toilsome walk if no boat was on hand to make the passage from the land. But Kate ran, careless of aching limbs, and surefooted on rocky faces which would have daunted her in more tranquil times. It is true, she slipped once or twice, and even tore her dress; she put a foot by mischance in a trapped pool and nearly fell, but none of these hazards halted her for long. Soon she was climbing the steep flight of steps which led to the high-placed door.

No one seemed to be about. She pushed it open tentatively, to reveal a spiral stair going directly up. Her echoes made a hollow noise in that chamber; she climbed with all the impetuosity that had brought her to the tower base, and hardly paused for breath as she burst into the room at the top.

It was the lighthouse keeper's living quarters, but something seemed not quite right. She had read, and always understood, that the light was tended night and day; that it was never left unguarded for fear that some stately ship of the Hemispheres might drive upon the rocks. But here was she, a stranger, able to walk into this enclosed world unchallenged. The sea was bright beyond the windows, but even in calm clear weather, surely the lighthouse should not have been left alone?

She looked about her to the circular room, which seemed as strongly built as a tomb chamber. Odd domestic details caught her eye. In one place stood a small gas cooker; further on, and ranged against the wall, was a narrow, single bed. To this she was drawn magnetically, and with growing dread, which reached a peak of alarm when she saw a figure lying motionless half under the coverlet. The sea breathed outside; she heard her own gasp of surprise; but no other sound broke the profound silence of the room. In the same instant she noticed a labelled bottle lying on its side on the table next to the bed, its cap off and its contents all gone. Her eyes flew back to the motionless figure.

Stealing forward, she saw that it was indeed Kathy, but a Kathy seemingly renewed, purged of the encrustations of sickness and decay. In her stillness, she seemed to have travelled back to the vivid beauty that had been hers the previous winter, when her skin had been pearly and firm, and her eyes danced with vital force. Alas! though, the eyes were wide open, they did not sparkle now; the cherry lips had a tint of sickly blue; death had sapped, had drained her face of colour.

Kate knelt down beside her and gently took her wrist, but she found no pulse. Tears sprang to her own eyes as she closed Kathy's, and mused on that disturbed spirit which had fled to a happier world. The empty bottle suggested—and it had not surprised her—that her distracted friend had taken her own life. Existence had been made insupportable to her long since by the machinations of those wretches in the cut-throat Northern Hemisphere.

She rose, sighing, and looked around the quiet room, in case Kathy should have left a note. There was nothing immediately apparent; still shocked and brooding, she began to open drawers and search through things. At one point, straightening up suddenly, she snagged the golden locket which she always wore, on a door handle, and the violent movement made the case spring open. She was grateful she had not broken the chain, and was about to shut it again when, to her astonishment, she saw that Kathy's photograph had disappeared, to be replaced by one of herself that dated from ten years ago. She remembered that photograph well; it had been taken by her father a few months before his death. What was mysterious was that it had never been in her possession; her father had packed it in his suitcase before he left their villa in Lancaster for the last time.

This occurrence made her fear for herself, and she closed the locket with tense, trembling fingers. Her fear was reinforced by the sudden tramp of footsteps on the staircase outside. She told herself that it must be the lighthouse keeper returning, and there was no need to panic. He would realise from the empty pill bottle that no murder had taken place, and that Kathy had taken her own life.

The footsteps drew to a halt. Kate tensed up as the door slowly creaked open; but it was all she could do to stop herself from crying out when she saw the lighthouse keeper's sinister appearance. He was wearing what appeared to be a balaclava helmet which concealed almost all of his face, except for his eyes. Almost noiselessly, he glided across the room, stopping within a few centimetres of the bed on which Kathy lay, lifeless. His eyes moved from that supine figure to Kate, arrested in shock; he gazed on her as if he could see into her soul. She stared back at him in perplexity; seeing the black hood and cloak with which his body was swathed.

"Kathy's committed suicide," she began faintly. "She's taken an . . . ."

The lighthouse keeper raised a veinless hand to indicate that she should remain silent. His finger went to his woolly lips and he slowly shook his head. Dazed by this, she could only think that he was a mute; or that he kept silent for some deeper reason. She forced herself not to retreat as he drew nearer to her, producing from the pocket of his gown a folded slip of paper, which he passed to her. She took it and fumbled as she opened it, her eyes still searching the masked face.

She glanced down. On the paper in large italic print was written:

> *"You must go now. Your friend is at peace. I will see to her. Return to the lighthouse at midnight. I will wait for you here in this very room."*

She folded the paper again and began edging back towards the door, but without taking her eyes off this mysterious figure for an instant.

"Why are you behaving like this?" she asked him, frowning. "Can't I at least see your face? How on earth can I communicate with you if you don't speak to me or show me what you look like?"

The lighthouse keeper understood and slowly discarded his hood. He removed his balaclava a few seconds later. Then indeed, Kate nearly swooned with astonishment, for the face that he revealed was none other than that of her father. It even wore the expression she remembered on the last night she had seen him, except that it was marked by ten years of ageing.

She began to feel delirious, as if her insides were being torn out; she leant up against the wall to stop herself from falling to the floor. For a few chaotic moments she saw nothing but blackness, as she suddenly felt everything slant and bowl over.

The she regained her vision and became aware that one half of the room had been replaced by the other in reverse, as if she were looking into a mirror. In the far corner, there now stood another bed with a table beside it; another body was lying lifeless on the counterpane. She drifted, stupefied, towards it to take a closer look. Whether or not her eyes were deceiving her, there was no way of knowing, but when she came within a few centimetres of the bed, she could clearly see that the figure on the coverlet was none other than a duplicate of her own.

Re-masking himself without expression, the lighthouse keeper pointed coldly to the door, signalling to Kate that she should go. And she did, but with drooping head, mournful rather than frightened now that the first shock had worn off. She left the room and made her way down the long, winding stair, with tears in her eyes at her friend's tragic fate; and quite convinced that she had seen the embodiment of her own yet to come.

Chapter Twenty-Six

Kate dragged her weary body home and entered the house. Her head was swimming; wherever she turned her eyes, she seemed to see Kathy's lifeless, virginal body stretched out. But something else caught her attention; it was a note on the kitchen table, haphazardly scrawled in Aunt Nancy's semi-literate hand:

> *"Kate—have gon too sea sisstar Rose for the day and tonite. Ther's a vegtable loaf inn the frig if yu wante it. Will bee bak tomorroe morenine. Yu've beene sente a letta froom Rebecca. It is onn the shelf abov the fyreplaice inn the lownge.*
>
> *"Aunt Nancy."*

She rose blindly from her seat and went into the lounge, and picked up the envelope with its crisp feel and its exotic stamp. Suddenly she found herself ripping it madly to get it open. She thought that nothing Rebecca could say could interest her much now:

"Dear Kate," (it began),

"It was so nice to see you at my wedding at the beginning of last month. Judah and I are most grateful to have received such lovely wedding gifts from yourself, your mother and Deborah. They are proving most useful at our villa in Lancaster.

"We enjoyed our honeymoon very much. We stayed at the 'Acropolis Hotel' in Athens, in the Eastern Hemisphere quarter of Greece; it was a splendid building which resembled a temple, with decorative stained glass windows. The first night we spent there holds a very special memory for both of us, for it was then that I conceived, if the doctor's calculations are correct. Isn't it wonderful news that I have become a mother-to-be already? Judah joins me in insisting that you come to our villa in Lancaster at the beginning of February when the baby is born. You must help us choose a name for it. We are already drawing up lists, but it's early days yet. We both hope that it will be a girl—to be educated, happily married and follow in her mother's footsteps. When she is strong enough to be able to use her hands, I will teach her how to draw and the theory of colour . . . ."

Kate folded the letter abruptly and slotted it back in its envelope. She could not bring herself to read any more; the carefully ornate handwriting seemed to make a mockery of Kathy's suffering. She snorted with a kind of helpless indignation at the injustices of this world, where one rides up smoothly as in a communal lift to the desired platform; and another, equally as gifted, and blessed with transcendent beauty, takes poison in the bitterness of her heart. And here, too, in this shabby Non-Hemisphere hovel, stood herself—an outcast, robbed forever of the cultured, artisan adulthood that she had so confidently anticipated.

It was a balmy day in June and the air was delirious even in this box of a house. Kate sensed as much, even while her thoughts were centred on the knowledge that an end must come. For her, she felt it was not far off. She returned to the kitchen and took pen and notepad from the cupboard. Soon, pushing her aunt's scrawl to one side, she was writing fluently her own note:

"Aunt Nancy,

"I thank you for being my companion and guardian over the past ten years; for feeding and guiding me, and providing a roof over my head when I was distraught and had nowhere to go. I am sorry that I was unable to put my education to much use in that I could not work for very long, or provide you with much money. I feel that in that respect I must have proved a burden to you at times."

"I know we have had our differences during the whole time I have lived in the Non-Hemisphere, but I feel that you are basically a decent, honest woman, who grew fond of me and showed concern for my welfare. I want you to realise this, Aunt Nancy, because as I write this, I fear that we must part.

"With all my love. Remember me.

"Kate."

She left the note on the table, laying the pen across it to prevent the fragrant summer breeze from sweeping it away. Scarcely had she done so than she heard footsteps in the hall. She looked up.

"The front door was open, so I came straight in." It was Bruce, but a contrite and respectful Bruce, very different from her last memory of him. "Kate," he said earnestly, "my wife and I have been discussing certain matters. We find that we are unable to agree on many of them, and that it is best that we should part. I have come back to you, Kate. I want you to be my wife."

What folly! She clutched at the locket, and it kept her safe. As if from far away she replied: "Kathy died, Bruce. She lost the fight; she took an overdose."

"How do you know?" he asked. "Did her mother tell you?"

"I found her body in the lighthouse this morning. There was an empty pill bottle beside her."

"Have the police been informed?" He looked puzzled, and yet sad, too.

"The lighthouse keeper told me he'd take care of it. Not that it makes much difference now. The time to have worried about Kathy was when . . ." She stopped, looking directly into his eyes for the first time since their fateful parting at his house long ago. "It was the Northern Hemisphere that ruined her, Bruce," she went on, in a tone that remained serene. "The callous attitudes of the people she worked for drove her to despair. She murdered a businessman's wife. It was her way of getting her revenge on those who had destroyed her."

"Murdered the innocent wife of someone she worked for?" exclaimed Bruce incredulously. "She actually took her revenge on someone she had never even met? The girl must have been out of her mind!"

Kate had been expecting some such response. The locket was cool in her hand; it encouraged her to reply in the same spirit.

"How can you imagine that we are compatible, Bruce, when you have a Northern Hemisphere occupation and have acquired Northern Hemisphere tastes; and I—a Non-Hemisphere down and out, like Kathy—was spat upon by your chosen associates and driven out of the environment in which you thrive? Do you suppose that things would change if I married you and came to live with you in a Northern Hemisphere home? Do you really think that this is what I would want after what your beloved quarter did to Kathy?"

"Kate, dear Kate," he said softly, "can't we put the past behind us? We have all suffered—Kathy, most of all—but you are young, and life is still sweet. Can't we make a fresh start, you and I?"

Kate's thoughts were drifting; fragments of diverse experience— Kathy lying dead; Rebecca nonchalant in her bridal dress—swam together, but it was Rebecca who swept serenely on. It was as if, from the beginning as children, Kathy, Rebecca and herself had been competing as to which one would live life to the full, and that eventually it was Rebecca who had prevailed. For that Kate found herself hating her, just as Kathy had hated the cosseted wife of the successful businessman. So it would go on; surgeon against clergyman; farmer against musician; down-trodden Non-Hemisphere victim against privileged Hemisphere lady; until the present structure of society had ceased to exist; and the steel barriers which permitted such iniquities were brought crashing down. For the work of the insulators had drastically misfired, she felt, and had done nothing but emphasise the tension between the classes. As for the sensitive under-age offenders, redistributed under the policy, the effect on them had been dire.

She remembered her late Eastern Hemisphere grandmother attending a party which her parents had arranged for her on the evening of her eighth birthday, held in a hired basilica situated within a few kilometres of their Lancaster villa. She recalled having sat quietly at her side, while the kindly grey-haired woman reminisced about her own childhood in the early twenty-first century, before society had been so drastically turned upside down.

In those days, urban and rural areas were scattered about the country under no particular zone. Her own mother, she told her, had trained as a draughtswoman at the Lancaster College of Art, but deciding that her chosen career did not appeal to her, she had become a secretary working for a firm of chartered accountants, just a few minutes' walk from where she lived. In that office, where she remained for many years, there were clerks with noticeable accents from the poorer parts of town, and other people from very different backgrounds; if they wanted to follow a path in life at variance with their parents' careers, they did so. Kate's grandmother told her how, on her way to school in the morning, she would pass her local church, and sometimes see the clergyman (who lived among them), striding across the churchyard in splendid religious vestments, which he made no attempt to hide.

Her closest school friend had been the daughter of a builder, and the two of them would laugh and play games at one another's house at weekends and in the school playground during lunch hours. It all seemed so quaint and long ago, that even as a child Kate had found herself smiling. The world class riots of 2030 had put a stop to all that. Whole cities had to be evacuated, their citizens being temporarily housed underground, while the process of separation was carried forward and the steel barriers were erected.

Kate's grandmother recalled how their family had endured three years of subterranean existence before they were admitted to the light again. By that time she was sixteen years old; having to wear the stola was the first big change she noticed.

As a member of the artisan race, she now found that there was no possibility of her becoming a white collar worker in a nearby office like her mother, all the offices in her neighbourhood having been demolished in accordance with the new policy. Her school friend, with whom she had been so close, was sent with her family to live in the Western Hemisphere quarter and they had soon lost touch; probably she would have become a transport worker or a domestic or blue collar worker. Such was the failed Utopian society into which Kate herself had been born; a society without compassion and unduly selective, whose unforgiving nature had caused the ruination of both Kathy and herself.

Bruce still stood a few paces from her. She drifted back to inhabit her frail body and heard herself replying flatly:

"You hurt me badly, Bruce." Her tone remained composed and without malice. "You rejected me as sexually inadequate, casting me off without regard to what would become of me. But don't think that yours was the only hurt I have had to endure. When I saw Kathy degenerating into the sad creature that she became, I saw a reflection of myself. My chance for happiness, the benefits of a good education; my strong ambition to become a musician; my hope of marrying and leading a fulfilled and normal life—all these things were thwarted because of one youthful indiscretion: a visit to a Farmlands nightclub, where all I did was sit at the bar and talk, like the millions of others who sit and talk every day, without considering that they are committing any crime. And what do I find to add insult to injury? My attacker escapes free, and I end up like Kathy—sexually destroyed.

"All this you know, but before we part, Bruce, I would like to say one thing more. Take care of your daughter. Guard her so that she doesn't fall a victim to this callous, class-conscious society, like Kathy and I did. Give her all your love, and let her mother do so, too, so that she does not go astray and then is forced to live apart as happened with my mother and me. I sincerely hope that she may grow up to find a changed society, where countries are undivided and where banishment for life is a punishment that no man or woman must endure."

She was moving down the hall and gliding towards the front door. She was leaving him behind.

"Kate," he pleaded as he saw her purpose, "please come back! You must not leave me. You have my word that I will not desert you if we make a second go of our relationship. I will be loyal to you forever."

The sea sang in her ears, blocking out his insubstantial voice. She turned back dreamily, already penetrated by a more powerful spirit. He seemed to flicker on the edge of dissolution, a figment of mere flesh. Stronger voices were calling her.

"If I should not return," she said, remembering the image of her body lying lifeless on the bed next to Kathy's, "tell Aunt Nancy that you were sorry for abandoning me, and that I forgave you for doing so. She's not a bad sort, deep down; if she knows that we made it all up in the end, she will let you into this house as a friend. Do this for my sake, Bruce; and by so doing, you will help to break down the barriers which stand between man and man. It is my only request to you."

And with that she ran out into the lane, moving with a light step. Bruce tried to follow, but he had no locket to pump its magic into his veins. He lost track of her within minutes.

Chapter Twenty-Seven

Kate made straight for the shore and the lighthouse steps. When she reached the door at their top, she found it open as before; it yielded to her and she passed inside. Still the locket seemed to fill her with its tireless energy; she glided up the long winding stair.

As she reached the entrance to the lighthouse keeper's quarters, she checked her watch again; and saw that the two hands were merging, coinciding over the Roman figure twelve, like human hands steeped in prayer. It was the hour of her meeting.

Here, too, all was as before at first glance, except that now a candle was flickering in the middle of the room. Its uncertain light made the shadows loom and chase, but it did reveal one change: Kathy's body had gone from the bed at the far side of the room, and another coverlet was spread there, which looked grey in the crescent moonlight.

A few metres to the right of the mahogany table, from which the empty bottle had also disappeared, a man silently sat with his back towards Kate; fearlessly she went forward. When he still did not turn, she gave a faint cough. Instantly he was on his feet and she was startled when she realised that he was no one she knew. This was a tall, thin man of about fifty, with a pinched looking face and narrow, deep-set eyes. The fierce hostility in his stance made her retreat a few paces and keep her distance.

"What the devil's this?" he finally said to her in a broad accent. "Who are you? What d'you think you're doing, breaking in here in the middle of the night?"

"I was looking for the lighthouse keeper," replied Kate, quelled a little by his harsh, unfriendly tone. "He told me to meet him up here at midnight. It's that now. Do you know where he is?"

He leant nearer, like a short-sighted man who has lost his glasses, trying to make her out. "What nonsense is this, young lady?" he said harshly. "There's only one lighthouse keeper on this coast, and that's me!"

"You can't be!" cried Kate, her eyes widening. "He was here earlier. He was wearing a black hood and a cloak."

"All right, that's enough—you've had your little joke," he replied. "There's no man in a hooded cloak here. Off you go now. It's not funny anymore."

She glanced uneasily towards the bed.

"Did you know a young girl called Kathy Fellowes?" she asked.

"Yes, she used to come up here quite often." The man was watching her warily now. "Why? What concern is that of yours?"

"I knew her, too," Kate replied. "She was my friend. She told me how she used to visit you in the lighthouse. She killed herself, didn't she? She was under severe mental strain."

His mood changed slightly. "Her body was removed this afternoon," he said. "Nothing can bring her back now. That's what comes of going out to work amongst those Northern Hemisphere folk." The light of resentment grew in his eyes as he spoke. "She'd have done better staying in the Non-Hemisphere where she belonged. I kept warning her what would happen when you try to cross the barriers in a society like this, but she was a stubborn young lady; she wouldn't hear any of it; and that wretched mother of hers kept tempting her with all those tales of what the Northern Hemisphere had to offer. If I had my way, I'd have the entire Northern Hemisphere wiped out. I'd like to put a bomb under the whole damn lot of them!"

Kate nodded slowly. There could be no doubt in her mind that this man was genuinely the keeper of the lighthouse and that the other, with whom she had made her tryst, was nothing more than a figment of her imagination.

"I share your view entirely," she said sadly, as she turned to make an exit. "We will all miss her. I'll go now."

She was as good as her word, turning quietly and making her way down the long, spiral stairway. When, however, she reached the last few steps, she glimpsed a shadowy, hooded figure out of the corner of her eye.

She pushed open the lighthouse entrance and felt a light rain falling; it had come on since she had entered the tower. All surfaces glittered in the wet, but the moon, her treacherous ally, had slipped behind a cloud and left the night confused.

She had to feel her way down the primitive, unlit steps, with no safety rail to lean upon. Suddenly the shore seemed a long way off. The sea was its old imperious self, dashing intermittently against the rocks and sending up a spray which wet her face. She stretched out both her arms like a bird in flight, in a feeble attempt to maintain her balance. Now the wind grew stronger and she was aware from high up, of the lighthouse beacon flashing out its warning to passing ships and setting the darkness back.

She was encouraged to raise one foot and reach down to the next tread. She slipped at once and went sprawling; a wave rolled over her and she was soaked through. Her hands fought the rock for a hold and found one; her feet wedged in a groove, but soon a larger wave pitched her off. Just as she was falling for the last time, the gloved hand of the rescuer reached out and lifted her up. Safely held, she glanced back briefly and was in time to see her own body plummeting into the raging, turbulent water.

She rose to her feet and found herself in a vast landscape, its hills and rivers without definite form or colour. Her father stood facing her; he had discarded his cloak and hood, along with the gloves he had been wearing when he had appeared on the rock. They turned to make their way down a shadowy, streamless dale, the rustling of leaves faintly audible as they walked. She felt utterly at peace without her shabby Non-Hemisphere dress; her father without his toga or helmet.

Far above them, silhouettes of fleeting birds glided gracefully in the daylight. They paused for a moment and looked up to watch them. One solitary bird slid smoothly over the Earth, which shone above the horizon, huge and bright.

Epilogue

Some homeless Non-Hemisphere inhabitants found Kate's body the next morning, washed up near the shore. It was laid to rest beside Kathy's, in a cemetery two kilometres from Terminal Lane.

Lonely and bereft, Kate's mother abandoned her Eastern Hemisphere villa to live with Deborah; as for Aunt Nancy, she spent the rest of her days in her house in Terminal Lane. Bruce returned to live permanently in the Eastern Hemisphere quarter, and became an instructor of athletics in a school not far from his new home. His family went with him; no divorce took place.

The locket, which was found on Kate, was sent by Aunt Nancy to Kate's mother. Mrs Tiberius decided to give it to Rebecca, who had been her daughter's dearest friend.

It was a mysterious item, that locket. Purchased in the Northern Hemisphere by a Non-Hemisphere inhabitant, and given to a

Hemisphere outcast as a gift. It now hung around the neck of one from the Eastern Hemisphere, gold returning to gold.

But Rebecca did not keep it for long. Within a few months of its passing into her possession, it was snatched from her amidst the bustle of her local electro-terminus, by a covetous, Non-Hemisphere inhabitant in a red disguisive mac.

The End